THE BETRAYAL OF DOCTOR VANE

When sisters Lydia and Janice Vane invited Giles Palmer to join their group practice Lydia was worried that he could prove dangerously attractive, but he was a good surgeon and would help to build up the practice the young women had taken over from their uncle. Giles found that while Janice was dynamic, Lydia seemed more of an enigma – she had a look of fear and sorrow for which her recent widowhood could not be totally responsible. Giles was right; there was a secret in Lydia's life – and it was mysteriously connected with her son Timothy.

m

THE BETRAYAL OF DOCTOR VANE

The Betrayal Of Doctor Vane

by

Sonia Deane

Dales Large Print Books
Long Preston, North Yorkshire,
BD23 4ND, England.

British Library Cataloguing in Publication Data.

Deane, Sonia
The betrayal of Doctor Vane.

A catalogue record of this book is available from the British Library

ISBN 1-84262-452-0 pbk

First published in Great Britain in 1978 by Hurst & Blackett Ltd.

Published in Large Print 2006 by arrangement with The estate of Sonia Deane, care of Rupert Crew Ltd.

Dales Large Print is an imprint of Library Magna Books Ltd.

Printed and bound in Great Britain by
T.J. (International) Ltd., Cornwall, PL28 8RW

1

Lydia Vane said, 'You probably think it strange that my sister and I want a surgeon to work with us in the practice, Dr Palmer.' She looked at Giles with directness.

'On the contrary; I'm counting on that fact to favour my application.' There was a whimsical note in his voice. 'I'm a physician as well as a surgeon, Dr Vane; so we should make a comprehensive group.' He did not remove his gaze from hers as he added, 'I understand that you are the senior partner, and that your sister takes care of obstetrics and family planning.'

A flicker of surprise crossed Lydia's face. 'News travels fast in Tewkesbury.'

'The information was given gratuitously when I asked to be directed here – to Prior's Gate.' He felt that she resented the possibility of gossip.

'I see… Are you married?' The question was asked hopefully.

'No.'

'Oh!'

'May I ask if you are?'

'I'm a widow, Dr Palmer.' She spoke quietly.

It was Giles' turn to say 'Oh!' adding swiftly, 'I'm sorry.' He became aware of her in that second. She was beautiful, with thoughtful grey eyes, and a haunting expression of sadness, which belied her cool efficient manner. It struck him that there was something a little mysterious about the set-up, although he had no justification for the conjecture. She was tragically young to be a widow, and hardly looked old enough to be a doctor. All the same, he knew that she must be about twenty-six or -seven, seeing that she had practised in Tewkesbury for three years.

In turn, Lydia was thinking that Giles Palmer might be dangerously attractive, and that an older, married man would be a wiser choice. As against that, she argued, she and her sister Janice wanted to build up the practice taken over from their uncle on his retirement, and even in these days good-looking doctors still held some inexplicable fascination for women. She excluded herself from the generalization, and playing for time until Janice could join them, introduced a lighter note by asking, 'You are not deterred by the prospect of working with two women?'

'Good lord, no! I'm accustomed to bossy females – they're part of hospital life!' He stopped, conscious of the indiscretion, and added apologetically, 'That was–'

'Honest,' Lydia cut in, 'and I know what you mean!'

'I'm here,' Giles assured her, 'because I want to work in general practice. The sex of my superiors is immaterial. Were you looking for an older, married man to join you?'

'That was in my mind.'

'Meaning that your sister does not support the idea?'

Lydia was faintly resentful of his questioning, but did not betray the fact as she replied involuntarily, 'Janice would be grateful not to have a partner's wife to consider.'

Janice Hunt came into the room at that moment, her gaze going straight to Giles. She was part rebel, part sophisticate, invariably succeeding in getting her own way. Her eyes were large, dark, and often mocking.

'Dr Palmer, I presume,' she said, appraising him boldly, then flashing Lydia a surreptitious approving glance.

Giles was amazed by the dissimilarity

between the two sisters, wondering if their relationship could possibly be harmonious, and feeling instinctively that if Janice didn't approve of him, his chances of coming to Prior's Gate were very slender. But after a general discussion, and learning that he was not married, she said confidently, 'We three should make an intriguing group practice.'

Lydia put in sharply, 'We're not aiming at being "intriguing", but at being good doctors, caring about our patients.' She paused, hating what must have sounded pompous. Her gaze met Giles' – a deep intent gaze that brought momentary silence.

Janie ignored the comment and said significantly, 'Two women and one man.' She savoured the prospect.

'Not an original situation,' Giles prompted. 'Merely that there are fewer practices with that permutation.'

'Then perhaps I should have used the words "less hackneyed" than the two-men-and-one-woman variety,' Janice persisted. Her expression was quietly triumphant. 'Has my sister told you about Noël Leigh?' she added swiftly.

Giles said, 'No,' and looked baffled.

Lydia hastened, 'Mr Leigh is a radiologist who has rooms in the old wing of Prior's

Gate. And while we work together he has nothing whatsoever to do with the practice.' She got up from her desk as she spoke. 'We'll be in touch with you, Dr Palmer.'

Giles had anticipated an immediate decision. Obtaining the position was not vital to him financially, or even from the point of view of ambition, and he had acted on impulse when applying for it, but now he was curious to know more about the two women facing him. They made the possible transition from hospital life to general practice a distinct challenge, because he sensed that Janice Hunt could be dynamite, while Lydia suggested the complete enigma.

'I shall be at the Hop Pole until the end of the week,' he said briskly, implying that he had no intention of hanging about while Lydia made up her mind.

Lydia realized that she had created an entirely wrong impression, but Janice's somewhat glib approach had irritated her, emphasizing the validity of her theory that an older, married man would be the wisest choice.

After Giles had left, Janice protested impatiently, 'Why couldn't you have agreed for him to join us? Why waste time on other applicants?' She added critically, 'Or are you still intent on getting some married monstrosity in his dotage?'

Lydia kept her temper, but her voice was resolute, 'I'm determined to avoid complications. And I certainly should not have made a decision without going thoroughly into the matter with you.' She paused, then, 'Obviously, Dr Palmer is an attractive man and–'

'Since when has that been a crime?' Janice cut in.

Lydia exclaimed in exasperation, 'Oh, don't be ridiculous!'

'Very well, then, I think he'll be a sensation with the patients ... what more do you want?'

'Peace of mind, and a climate in which to run and build up a good practice.' Perplexity clouded Lydia's eyes, 'And if we cannot talk rationally, what hope is there for the future?'

Janice lowered her gaze. She felt contrite, rebellious and frustrated, but her attitude was conciliatory as she pointed out, 'Dr Palmer didn't get his degrees on the strength of his *looks*, and you could tell by the way he spoke that this appointment was by no means vital to him.'

Lydia was unable to account for the presentiment which warned her against becoming involved with Giles Palmer, while in no way personally opposed to him. Nevertheless she capitulated, 'Then we agree about his joining us.'

Janice's smile was slow. She oozed satisfaction.

'Certainly.'

Lydia stifled her misgivings as she said, 'I think we should stress that we want a future partner, not someone who is likely to move on just when we think we're settled.'

'I couldn't agree more!' Janice exclaimed. 'We've had enough assistants who turned out to be a pain in the neck.'

'That brings us to the question of the cottage … do we offer it to him? To rent, of course.'

'The *cottage!*' There was surprise and doubt in Janice's voice.

'Well, it's empty at the moment, and that's a hazard in these days.' Lydia looked at Janice, sensing her antipathy to the suggestion, and hastening, 'But if you'd rather–'

'No! No; I think it a good idea now that the Morgans have gone to Australia. We don't need it. Heaven knows this place is large enough.' Janice's views were crystallizing as she spoke, 'But he may already have furniture of his own, or even a *place* of his own.'

'That remains to be seen,' Lydia said in business-like fashion, adding as an afterthought, her expression suddenly dubious, 'Although there's such a thing as being–'

'Too close,' Janice put in swiftly, and on a note of banter which concealed ridicule. 'He'd certainly have to be a superman ever to get close to *you,* so I shouldn't worry on that score.'

Lydia ignored the remark, but her lips tightened.

Janice rushed on, 'Are you going to telephone him?'

'Yes.'

'This evening?'

'Possibly; and I shall be late for supper, so don't wait for me. I've a visit after surgery – Mrs Monk.'

'Then why not look in at the Hop Pole and *see* Dr Palmer? After all, Mrs Monk lives within a stone's throw of that place.'

'I shall not do that.' Lydia was emphatic. 'And there's just one other thing–' She gave Janice a penetrating warning look. 'I want our respective relationships with Dr Palmer to be conducted on a strictly professional basis. This will be a new experience for both of us, and mixing business with pleasure seldom works.'

Colour rushed to Janice's cheeks, her temper flared, 'You can't dictate to me, *or* to Dr Palmer, as to how we conduct our social life. Just because you're determined to live without emotion or sexual contact is no reason why you should impose the penalty on others. You may be the senior partner, but once I've fulfilled my obligations to my patients, I'm entitled to do as I please.' Anger choked her as she added, 'And let me tell *you* something: at this rate you'll become a frigid pompous bore!' With that, she flounced from the room.

Lydia remained seated at her desk. She was trembling and her nerves left raw. She winced as the word 'frigid' echoed distastefully, and now she deplored the fact that she had ever considered taking a man as a future partner. In addition, she realized that her greatest folly lay in having deluded herself that she and Janice could ever work harmoniously together. Unfortunately, the decision to do so had been made at a time of emotional stress when her judgement was impaired. A sigh escaped her; she felt like someone sitting alone in a room that was gradually, insidiously, being blocked up, brick by brick, shutting her out of the world, and defying all possible means of escape.

The intercom went, making Lydia jump, but alerting her to the appointments.

Jane Mason, the practice secretary, said, 'Mrs Easton has just arrived.'

A few seconds later Lydia extended a welcoming hand to the patient who brought with her a suggestion of lavender and lace.

'I hate troubling you,' came the familiar apology – mostly from patients who were very considerate.

Lydia reassured her. Mrs Easton practised a brand of medicine originated by her mother, clinging to the old wives' tales, while just conceding that a doctor *was* sometimes necessary. On this occasion she came to the point, 'I'm not feeling well, Dr Vane; not well at all.'

Lydia gave her a thorough examination, and when she'd finished and Mrs Easton was dressed again, and back in the consulting room, Lydia said, 'I want to get you X-rayed... Mr Leigh will–'

'X-rays!' The word was uttered with dread and faint disapproval.

Lydia smiled. 'You *did* have a bad pleurisy a year or so ago, and–'

'Oh, you mean that the pain in my chest

has something to *do* with the pleurisy?' There was relief in the rush of words.

Lydia had counted on that reaction, and relied on her smile to avoid a direct answer, as she hastened, 'I'll get my secretary to make an appointment with Mr Leigh … tomorrow sometime,' she added.

'In the afternoon,' came the thin voice. 'My sister and I always take Daniel for a walk in the morning. Such good exercise, my mother always used to say.'

Lydia humoured her, calculating that the mother would be at least a hundred and fifty by now! She did not stress that Noël Leigh was always heavily booked up, but because he was on the premises Jane Mason managed to twist his arm.

'Two-thirty,' Lydia said finally.

Mrs Easton repeated the time, adding, 'I don't think I shall go for a walk tomorrow morning, after all. I found it very tiring this morning – very tiring. That was really what made me come to see you, Dr Vane. I've always loved walking.' She looked at Lydia hopefully.

'Then we must get you well enough to enjoy it again.'

Mrs Easton's voice broke as she said, much to Lydia's surprise, 'You're such a tower of strength. I don't know what I should do without you.' With that, Mrs Easton went away, and Jane Mason took her place in Lydia's consulting room.

'Any time for a mere secretary? We must get these reports done.' Jane was an auburn-haired, bright girl, efficient and humorous, whose love-life resembled a computer fed with the wrong data. She had great affection and respect for Lydia, while feeling that there was some dark secret in her life which prevented close friendships, and made medicine both her profession and hobby. She seldom spoke, Jane reflected, of her late husband, although it was natural to assume that his death had been an irreparable loss. 'Shall we start with Mrs Grantham?' Jane added.

Lydia nodded. Investigation had revealed an inoperable growth, and the case had to be referred to a physician in Bath, where the Granthams had moved to be near their respective parents. When the report was finished, Lydia sighed and sat back in her chair. There was a momentary silence. Mrs Grantham was only forty-eight.

'When are you going on holiday, Dr Vane?' Jane spoke abruptly, but with solicitude. 'You badly need a break.'

‘I’ll think about it when Dr Palmer has settled in.’

‘Oh! So you’ve decided on him?’

‘Yes.’

Jane beamed. ‘If his ability matches his good looks our troubles should be over! I only saw him just as Una admitted him. Struck me as the strong authoritative type – just what we need.’ She hastened, ‘Oh, not because you and Dr Hunt–’

‘I know what you mean,’ Lydia cut in, smiling. ‘A question of a man about the practice! Our last assistant hardly qualified for the role, I admit.’

Jane beamed again. To her, Giles Palmer was dishy – someone she could fall for in a big way, to use her own terminology.

Lydia took surgery alone that evening, and when the last patient had gone, went to see Mrs Monk, deciding to have a meal out and a walk by the river. Solitude didn’t worry her; in fact she preferred it to disharmony, because Janice in her present mood could create an impossible atmosphere without uttering a word.

Tewkesbury lay golden in the June sun as Lydia reached its old streets with their timeless beauty. Mrs Monk was eighty-four and lived over a shop near the Hop Pole.

She suffered with chronic emphysema but managed to cope with the aid of social workers, who loved her, and Lydia regarded her as a friend. Judith Monk had 'seen better days' but did not resent their passing, neither did she bore those around her by boastful reminiscences.

'You shouldn't come to see me on a lovely evening like this, Dr Vane… I'm really quite well, considering.' She spoke between gasps as she made her way, breathlessly and painfully, to her chair after admitting Lydia. Her hands were gnarled and misshapen with arthritis, but her wrinkled-apple face was bright and there was still a twinkle in her eyes which once had been large and beautiful. Her judgement was perceptive, and she had decided that Lydia was far from happy and that there was something about her which did not wholly conform to the pattern of grief.

'"Considering", being the understatement of the year,' Lydia quipped as she finally closed her medical bag, having gone through the routine of temperature, respiration and blood pressure.

'I want to live another two months,' came the brisk announcement. 'My son's coming home from South America. He'll be sixty-two in August. I haven't seen him for three years.' A croaking chuckle followed. 'So you see, you *must* keep me alive, Dr Vane!'

'I don't like being restricted to two months or two years,' Lydia retorted, smiling as she spoke, but doubtful that Judith Monk would survive even until August, and more than ever perturbed because she lived alone. Yet it was unthinkable that she should be put into a home. She was neither senile, nor incontinent, but there was the ever present danger of heart failure. A son of sixty-two, Lydia mused, as she left the flat and walked blindly along the street towards her car. Suddenly she heard her name called, and turned to face Giles Palmer.

'That was a real trance,' he said wryly.

Lydia didn't deny it.

'But you *do* know who I am?'

She was suddenly aware of him as she raised her gaze and murmured, 'Of course!'

'May I suggest you come in and have a drink with me?' he asked hesitantly, indicating the hotel entrance as he spoke.

Her first instinct was to refuse and then, realizing that she would have to communicate with him, his invitation provided a good opportunity. They went straight through to the cocktail bar and sat overlooking the garden. The moment seemed completely unreal to her; as though she had been transported through time and space into an entirely different world. A few seconds later he raised his sherry glass and, looking straight into her eyes, said, 'I'm very grateful for your trance, otherwise you might have *seen* me, and looked the other way!'

'That assumption being incorrect,' she said.

'Oh!'

'I was going to telephone you; now it will not be necessary.'

He nodded, preparing himself for rejection, and conscious of unexpected disappointment at the prospect.

Lydia took a deep breath, feeling uneasy and nervous, but her voice was firm, even brisk, 'My sister and I would like you to join us.'

Enthusiasm gave emphasis to his spontaneous, 'I couldn't be more pleased.'

They looked at each other, smiling; both equally surprised by their reactions. For a second there was silence, which Lydia broke, her gaze intent, 'I'm glad you don't want to escape the frustrations of the N.H.S., *or* leave the country.'

'I happen to love England,' he said simply.

'The Cotswolds in particular,' he added with feeling. 'I'm always drawn back here.'

A shadow crossed her face. 'Meaning that you have lived in this area before?'

He sensed her apprehension.

'No; merely visited... I've an aunt who has a week-end cottage at Ledbury.' He held her gaze. 'And you? Is this your home ground?'

'Up to a point,' she replied evasively, hurrying on, 'Have you any plans, so far as living accommodation is concerned? I take it you have a flat in London?'

He felt that her questions concealed an inner anxiety, quite apart from their validity. He explained that he had a rented furnished flat not far from the B.B.C., which he could easily vacate. 'I've been determined not to dig any roots until I found the right place for them.'

'And *is* this the right place, Dr Palmer? We want someone who will stay with the view to becoming our partner.'

He looked at her with a penetrating, searching intensity, 'Oh, yes,' he said, his deep voice enriching his words, 'this is the right place. I can assure you of that, and of my enthusiasm for a possible partnership at some future date. I liked your idea of building up the practice for the benefit of the patients, instead of being content with shoddy medicine, merely for financial gain.' A wry smile touched his lips, 'Not that we don't all need money, but it doesn't have to be our sole objective in life.'

Something in his manner and expression stimulated her eagerness and a tremor of emotion touched her – emotion suddenly new and exciting after the sterile years. Nevertheless, panic built up as she felt his gaze upon her, and she looked away, scared by her own vulnerability.

Giles was baffled by what seemed her unexpected withdrawal as she said formally, 'I'm sure we shall work harmoniously together.' Her vice shook; she resented the weakness because she was seeing Giles not merely as a doctor vital to the practice, but as a man she found overwhelmingly attractive, both mentally and sexually. Yet she hardly knew him, she argued, struggling to change her mood. And *she* was the one who had insisted that the relationship was to be strictly professional!

'Dr Vane,' Giles said softly, 'you've gone into that trance again ... it intrigues me.'

'I'm sorry.' Lydia sighed, squared her shoulders, nerving herself to meet his gaze as she hurried on, 'Since you haven't a permanent home, would you care to have the cottage that belongs to Prior's Gate? Originally, it was the Lodge, but the property has changed so much since my uncle bought it many years ago, that we regard it as the Cottage. It has been modernized and well equipped, and while it is furnished, there is plenty of space for any of your personal belongings.'

There was a second of appreciative assessment before Giles said, 'That would be marvellous.' He looked delighted.

Lydia hurried on, trying to sound calm and matter-of-fact, 'At least it would enable you to look around–'

'Meaning that the arrangement would be temporary?'

'Not unless you wished it to be. I was merely allowing for your not finding it suitable. We've been letting it furnished, and the previous tenants vacated it just recently... I know it is very near Prior's Gate, but not overlooked by it!'

'I think that being on the spot is a great asset,' he said stoutly. He glanced at his watch. 'And now will you stay and have dinner with me?'

Caution, discretion, urged her to decline; desire, excitement, the sudden feeling of having been swept back into life, made her accept. Her heart was racing; she was conscious of his every movement; almost painfully aware of him. It was a very long while since she had dined alone with a man, she thought self-consciously, having always refused to get involved, or to allow friendships to deepen. At this moment will power deserted her and a few minutes later, they went into the dining room as though their being together was the most natural thing in the world.

When coffee was reached, Giles said sombrely, 'You are an enigma, Dr Vane.' Tension mounted as he continued to look at her intently, 'One day you may care to tell me just a *little* about yourself,' he added, his voice low and full of emotion.

Lydia averted her gaze and then said quietly, 'Why perpetuate unhappiness by dwelling on it?'

His eyes met hers, searching, seeking an explanation which he knew would be denied him, 'Because I feel that unhappiness doesn't tell the whole story,' he announced with perception.

A waiter approached the table, well aware of Lydia's identity. She was wanted on the telephone.

Janice said with faint cynicism, 'I *thought* I

should find you if I rang the hotel… I didn't believe for a second that you really intended *telephoning* Dr Palmer. Sorry to interrupt your little tête-à-tête… Mrs Monk has collapsed; a neighbour in the flat below rang. Better get across to her.' With that the line went dead.

Annoyance mingled with Lydia's concern as she hurried back to Giles and explained the situation.

'Can I be of help?' he asked.

Lydia glanced at him, grateful for the offer. 'I'd be glad if you'd come along with me.'

But Mrs Monk was dying. She recognized Lydia in that last second of consciousness, and whispered *'August.'*

It was later at the hotel, over a much-needed brandy, that Giles asked, 'What did August mean?' He studied Lydia's pale, sad face as he spoke.

Lydia explained, adding, 'She was a brave woman. I shall miss her; she put up a magnificent fight to stay alive until her son returned… Now I feel guilty, almost responsible, if you like.'

'Good heavens, why? Nothing could possibly have been done to save her.'

'I didn't mean that. I ought to have insisted that she went into a home of some sort; but she was so against it; so independent. I'd comforted myself that when her son returned the problem could be dealt with–' Lydia stopped and looked at Giles appealingly, 'but I didn't really believe she could last until then.'

He said gently, 'I'm sure your patient would have chosen to die in her own bed rather than in a strange home, or hospital.'

Lydia nodded her agreement.

'We all know how impossible it is to judge the time factor. We have no contract with death to simplify our job. I'm sure you did everything possible for her.'

'I tried to do so,' Lydia admitted, comforted by Giles' presence and his quiet strength which reassured her. It was a very long while since she'd been able to share a burden, and again a tremor of emotion touched her; this man sitting beside her was no longer a stranger; no longer merely the man chosen as future partner, but someone inexplicably bound up with her personally, in a relationship which already might have spanned years. She trembled, not through nervousness, but because excitement brushed aside even grief, drawing them together in what they both recognised as physical, and mental, attraction.

'It's difficult,' she managed to say, 'not to get involved with patients.'

He held her gaze, 'Even friendship, without involvement, is sterile.'

Again they looked at each other and continued to look, in silence, then Lydia said in a breath, 'I must get back.'

'I suppose so.' There was a grudging note in his voice.

They went out into the summer night; the streets were empty of traffic, but filled with soft blue shadows and a strange peace. It was still warm, and Lydia felt the breeze on her cheeks, shivering with a sudden sharp awareness of beauty, and overwhelming emotion.

Giles looked down at her as she got into the car, and settled in the driving seat.

'We haven't arranged when I am to start at Prior's Gate.'

'I'll leave it to you.'

'Tomorrow.' He added urgently, because he didn't want to be put off, 'I could ease myself in; be of some use, and–'

Lydia interrupted, 'You will also have to make sure that the cottage is suitable.'

'It will be.' He spoke with finality.

'Very well… Good night, Dr Palmer.'

'Until tomorrow, about eleven,' he said,

his gaze holding hers.

The sound of his voice re-echoed as Lydia drove away, and thought after thought tumbled through her mind. There was so much she had to tell him; so much she did not want to tell him; nevertheless some strange alchemy had drawn them together that night and, as a result, life had acquired a new dimension. But as the car stopped at Prior's Gate, reality crushed her as she contemplated meeting Janice's critical, observant gaze.

'Well?' Janice exclaimed, studying Lydia intently as she entered the hall.

'Mrs Monk died.' Lydia walked ahead into the high-ceilinged old-fashioned drawing room.

'Really! Judging from your flushed face and happy expression, I assumed you'd managed to save her.'

'I cannot grieve because Mrs Monk's suffering is over; only that she did not live to see her son.'

'A natural reaction,' Janice mocked, still staring at Lydia with penetrating directness. 'And Dr Palmer? What had you to say to each other all this time?'

'All that was necessary,' came the brief reply. 'He is anxious to join us right away, and will be very glad to have the cottage.'

'I don't doubt *that.*' There was grievance in the remark.

Lydia felt angry. 'I asked you about his having the cottage and you agreed that it was a good idea.'

Janice shrugged her shoulders and then added darkly, 'It probably is. We can always get him out in an emergency.'

'Why should there be an emergency?'

'Your guess is as good as mine; but it has been known… Glad you had such an obviously pleasant evening. Don't bother to lay down any more rules about strictly professional relationships.' A scowl spread over Janice's face. '*Telephone* him! You–'

'I almost collided with Dr Palmer outside the hotel,' Lydia cut in icily, 'otherwise I should certainly not have seen him this evening; and if you're going to begin by making trouble–'

Janice laughed tauntingly as she walked to the door. '*Then* what will you do? Good night, dear sister,' she added.

The following morning Giles studied Prior's Gate with a new interest. A gabled Cotswold-stone house, standing slightly back from the road, the cottage nearby – approached from a side-turning – was partly ringed by an orchard which gave it complete seclusion. When Giles swung his car into the short drive of Prior's Gate, he sat for a second contemplating its picturesque rose-filled garden, feeling both delightful and exhilarated. A small boy ran across the lawn, an adult at his heels, and seeing Giles, hesitated, smiled, and disappeared from sight.

Janice appeared on the front doorstep. 'Hello,' she called brightly, and extended a welcoming hand as Giles reached her. 'My sister's had to rush off to a suspected appendix, and asked me to show you around. She wondered if you might like to go over the cottage.'

Giles' enthusiasm waned; he'd been looking forward to seeing Lydia.

'We can walk through the orchard,' Janice went on, indicating a small iron gate nearby. 'Although we cannot actually see the cottage except in winter, when the trees are bare, it is conveniently near.'

Giles looked around him appreciatively. 'This is a beautiful spot… By the way, who was the child I saw running across the lawn just now?'

'Oh, that was Timothy,' Janice said blandly. 'Didn't Lydia tell you about him? He was born after her husband died.'

2

Lydia glanced at her watch as she left the Melrose house, thankful that Andrew Melrose had nothing more serious than a bad bilious attack, and not appendicitis as his parents had feared! With luck she would get back to Prior's Gate well before Giles Palmer arrived. She particularly wanted to show him over the cottage herself, and could not suppress the excitement building up within her at the prospect of seeing him again. *Again!* When she had met him only for the first time yesterday! Colour rushed to her cheeks; but she was deaf to reason which warned her that she was thinking and behaving like an infatuated adolescent. *Infatuated.* The word did not ring true, and she dismissed it. For all that, she felt at one with the sunlit day, the sweet fragrance of summer, and the beauty of the countryside around her, with Bredon Hill etched in faint purple against a taut blue sky. Janice had said that she would be at the clinic until midday, and she, Lydia, had briefed Una to deal with any telephone calls, and to offer Giles Palmer a coffee should he be early. The car purred as she turned down the bylane which would take her past the cottage. She would make sure that everything there was in order, and a bubble of happiness touched her as she drew onto the grass verge and then made her way to the front door which, to her dismay, was open. The panic lasted only a second, for Janice called out, 'We're here, Lydia. I heard your car.'

Lydia stepped into the miniature hall, trembling.

'Good morning, Dr Vane,' Giles said politely.

'Good morning,' she echoed, her voice flat.

Janice looked very pleased with herself. 'Our partner-to-be is delighted with the place. Yes, *Giles?*' She stressed the Christian name which she had subtly introduced, suggesting that, since they were to work together, formality was absurd.

'Most certainly. It is delightful. When the apple trees are actually in bloom it must be a magnificent sight.'

Lydia, struggling to conceal her disappointment and frustration, nodded, and then said to Janice, 'I thought you had a clinic this morning.'

'I have.' Janice smiled. 'But not until later.'

All Lydia's plans, her intentions, had been thwarted; she stood there bleak, vulnerable, while conscious of a subtle change in Giles' manner. Actually, Giles was completely mystified by Timothy's advent. Surely it would have been the most natural thing in the world for Lydia to have mentioned him? Also, he was baffled by Janice's request that he should not disclose the fact that he knew about the child, in case Lydia might misunderstand. Why, he argued, in heaven's name, should a mother misunderstand anything connected with her own son? It struck him that his first reaction to Lydia had obviously been the correct one. She *was* an enigma.

The house telephone rang – an internal line between Prior's Gate and the Cottage. It was for Janice. Una told her that one of her patients was haemorrhaging and would she go at once? Janice frowned, explained, and hurried away.

Giles and Lydia stood in silence for a second, each wanting to recapture the magic of the previous night.

'I'm glad you like the cottage,' Lydia said tritely, her gaze meeting his, and then lowering shyly.

'It's ideal. I am singularly fortunate.' His voice was pleasant. He was stating facts. 'The view beyond the orchard–'

'Right to Bredon Hill.' She rushed on, 'I'm sorry I wasn't here when you arrived, I wanted–'

'That's all right,' he said formally, 'your sister told me you'd suggested that I might like to look over the cottage–'

'But–' Lydia stopped; she could hardly emphasize that she had not said anything of the sort.

Timothy and his Nanny crossed the orchard at that moment, out for their usual morning walk. Lydia's heart missed a beat; she was conscious of Giles studying her intently. She hastened, 'That's Timothy… I should have mentioned him last night; but somehow–' She made a little gesture to suggest that she'd overlooked many things. 'He's – he's my son.' She spoke with a strange inevitability. 'He was born after Dennis, my husband, died.'

Giles did not quite know why he had felt so resentful of the child when Janice had spoken of him. Was it because his presence seemed a completion of Lydia? Or merely that he felt she might have taken him into her confidence more fully? Yet why should she? The idea, at that moment, became an arrogance he regretted, annoyed by his own aberration. Suddenly there seemed something stark, even tragic, in her simple announcement, and he wondered what heartache and suffering lay behind it. 'Dennis, my husband.' And as Giles stood there he had the unreasonable feeling of outrage because she had been married; because another man had already shared her life. His nerves were taut; an explosive jealousy racked him.

'I'm – I'm sorry,' he managed to say in a strangled voice.

'You seem shocked,' Lydia challenged.

'Without the slightest justification,' he apologized.

'Are you allergic to children?'

'Good lord, no!'

'I assure you that my home life is never mixed with my professional,' she flashed at him with faint austerity. 'You will not be regaled with stories about Timothy; what he does, says, or how clever he is.' She stopped because she realized she was making out a case, *explaining*, to mollify Giles; and she shuddered at her own involvement.

He said quietly, 'I was thinking how much you must have suffered.'

Lydia did not deny it.

They remained standing in the sunlit sitting room, the fragrance from lavender hedges in the small garden wafting on the warm breeze; the silence broken only by bird song.

'Work!' Lydia cried suddenly, as though it were a foreign word. *'Patients!'*

'Reality,' he murmured, taking a last look at what was soon to be his home.

'You can have the keys,' Lydia said as they left, 'and rearrange the furniture to allow for your own things... Now come and meet Noël Leigh; we try to manage a coffee about this time, and discuss any problems.'

'Very handy to have a radiologist on the spot.'

'Speeds things up and helps diagnosis,' she agreed. 'As well as saving patients a great deal of trouble.'

Noël Leigh greeted Giles with reserve, opposed to his joining the Prior's Gate practice because, being in love with Lydia, he hated the possibility of a rival. Noël was a tall impressive figure whose attitude towards Lydia was both possessive and protective. He spoke with a proprietory air as he addressed Giles, 'I've been very anxious for Dr Vane to have the right permanent help. She works far too hard.' He managed subtly to convey that he had reservations about her choice of a future partner.

'I've hardly done that this morning,' Lydia flashed, 'but this is the exception, Dr Palmer. Things are usually pretty hectic.'

'We were not exactly idle at the hospital,' Giles exclaimed, 'so pressure of work will not be new.' He looked at Noël, 'You have splendid equipment here.'

Noël relaxed slightly. 'We pride ourselves on the best.' He flashed Lydia a little significant smile. 'Don't we?' he added.

Lydia felt slightly uncomfortable. 'This is entirely your domain, Noël. I don't come into it, except where my patients are concerned.'

Noël said airily, 'Dr Palmer will not believe that.'

Dulcie Reed, one of Noël's radiographers, and a general factotum, appeared with coffee. Giles watched the way her gaze darted suspiciously from Noël to Lydia, her jealousy obvious. In that second he felt he was looking at the pieces of a jigsaw puzzle without having any idea what the picture was likely to be.

Lydia, faintly irritated by Noël's attitude, made an excuse to leave immediately after the coffee was drunk, indicating that Giles could make himself known to Jane and Una, while she saw a patient now due.

'And don't forget, Lydia,' Noël said as she and Giles reached the door, 'that you're dining with me tonight, and that we've to get to Stratford in time for the theatre.'

Lydia had forgotten, and she flushed slightly, but assured him that she would be ready as early as patients permitted.

'And I don't want to *know* about patients!' He was adamant. 'Insist on Janice being on call for a change.' He beamed at Giles, suddenly expansive. 'With you around, things will be simpler.'

'Noël,' Lydia explained, as she and Giles went through to the main building, 'was here in my uncle's time.'

'An old friend?' Giles hinted.

'You could say that.'

Later on, Giles had reason to recall the remark. At that moment, however, he asked, 'Could I be of help this evening?'

'Thank you all the same, but Janice will take surgery.' Lydia felt awkward, but determined that Janice should not initiate him into practice methods. 'And I'd rather you familiarize yourself with the layout here; have a word with Jane and Una, as I've already said.'

There was a sudden silence. Giles broke it on a note of interrogation, 'Are you having seconds thoughts about my joining you, Dr Vane?'

Lydia panicked. There was a tightness in her throat, and she was trembling. It was absurd to be so affected by this man; absurd and dangerous. She wanted stability in the practice, but if she could not control her emotions, what hope had she of achieving her objective?

'No; no,' she hastened.

'Then I'll do as you say,' he agreed formally.

'Dr Palmer?'

'Yes?'

She floundered and opened a door to her left, 'This will be your consulting room. Una will tell you anything you want to know about the files and instruments.'

He nodded. 'Then I'll see you on Monday next. Meanwhile, before I go to London at the week-end, I'll prepare the cottage – make way for my belongings … what about returning the keys?'

'Just leave them at Prior's Gate,' Lydia said easily. 'We've a housekeeper, Mrs Lane and her husband, who live on the premises.'

'I'll get back on Sunday, earlyish, finally to

settle in.'

Lydia smiled. 'A good idea.'

'Will you be at home?'

'Probably.' She stiffened. 'Why?'

He had been going to suggest a drink, but thought better of it.

Something in his manner, the way he looked at her, made her say involuntarily, 'Why not come to supper around seven-thirty? We shall need to talk anyway.'

He held her gaze. 'I'd like that … thank you.'

Lydia left him and hurried into her consulting room. Why ask him to supper? True, there were things to be discussed, but she'd merely acted on a foolish impulse.

At that moment Una showed the patient in, and Lydia concentrated immediately on the young girl who finally sat down, facing her.

'I think I'm pregnant again, Dr Vane.'

'Then,' Lydia said gently, 'it is my sister you need to see, Mrs Templeton.'

'No; no, I don't.' The words came breathlessly and with decisiveness. 'Dr Hunt hasn't any time for me because I refused to keep on the Pill.' A pleading note came into Madge Templeton's voice, 'After all, you looked after me when I had pneumonia last year.'

'That was quite different,' Lydia pointed out. 'I have nothing to do with obstetrics. My sister is completely in charge.'

'But she doesn't *understand.* The Pill upsets me. And my husband isn't happy about my taking it. I've tried several types, or whatever you call them. I'm so irregular that other methods don't seem to work, either.' She stopped and made a helpless gesture, waiting for Lydia to speak.

But Lydia was angry. Janice had no right to create such apprehension in a patient, or place her at such a disadvantage.

'Let me see,' Lydia prompted encouragingly, 'how many children have you now?'

'Four ... this will be the fifth.' She looked down at her hands which were tightly clasped, and then raised her gaze to meet Lydia's. 'We've been married five years. Dr Hunt warned me last time about having another baby.'

'That was for the sake of your health,' Lydia suggested.

'I know; but I just can't *face* her.'

And while Lydia was aware of the fanciful, or moody, phases of pregnancy, she realized that it would take more than a few soothing phrases to counteract this deep-rooted antagonism.

'Then I think I'll have a word with my sister – unless of course you would prefer to transfer to another doctor?'

'Oh, no! I don't want to register with anyone else. I just wish *you* could look after me.'

Lydia reiterated that to do so was not possible, adding, 'But if I may discuss your case with my sister, I'm sure we could arrive at an understanding.'

Fear widened Madge Templeton's round blue eyes.

'I could never have a – a termination,' she exclaimed feverishly.

'Good heavens, that was the last thing in my mind,' Lydia assured her. 'Suppose you make an appointment with Dr Hunt tomorrow, and I'll talk to her beforehand.'

'If you would… I'm being very silly, I know. But I hate feeling, well, *guilty,* because I don't do as she advises. My husband and I love children,' she rushed on defensively.

Lydia tackled Janice later that day, and for once did not receive a diatribe.

'My concern for Mrs Templeton was purely professional. I'm worried about her,' Janice insisted. 'She and her husband are prejudiced against the Pill and she's not very good with other contraceptives. She'd had three difficult births before she came to me, and I wanted to have her sterilized after the fourth arrived. I'm alarmed by the possibility of yet another pregnancy, and I doubt very much if she'll go to term, in which case it will have to be a hysterectomy, which in the circumstances would be her salvation. She's twenty-five and already has four children!'

Lydia appreciated the point of view. 'Just so long as you don't appear critical.'

Janice sounded convincing as she said, 'That's the last thing: if she *is* pregnant again, it could be dangerous. I'll do my best to reassure her, of course. *And* watch her like a hawk!'

'Splendid.' Lydia was thankful for the co-operation.

'Giles was more than delighted with the cottage,' Janice exclaimed irrelevantly.

'I know.'

'He called me in just now to see how he had rearranged the furniture in the sitting room. An improvement, too. Apparently he has a grandmother clock he wants to bring... Oh, he told me you'd invited him to supper on Sunday.'

'Yes.'

Janice looked at Lydia very levelly, 'I was

to have gone over to Evesham to the Bartlets', but I shall put them off. I'd like to be in on any little talk you and Giles have. Unless you deliberately chose to have an *a deux* meal, and I should be in the way. I must say, your change of heart is intriguing.'

Lydia wanted to make some explosive retort, but was in no mood for argument. All she said was, 'I hadn't any idea that you were going to the Bartlets'... By the way, I'll leave the numbers of our seats at the theatre, and we shall have dinner at the Shakespeare Hotel, so should there be any dire emergency tonight–'

Janice cut in, 'You forget that Giles is in Tewkesbury – more than ready to help out, so no need to worry.'

Lydia felt a pang and said rather severely, 'I'd rather Dr Palmer was not troubled, and–'

Again Janice interrupted, 'Oh, don't be so stuffy ... and have a good evening. Why you haven't gone out with Noël before baffles me. He's mad about you.'

Lydia gasped, 'Don't be ridiculous.'

Janice scoffed, 'Don't *you!*'

'I don't want myths built up around my relationships,' Lydia insisted.

Janice laughed outright. 'My dear Lydia

you yourself are a myth … nothing real about you. My sympathies are with Noël.' She shook her head as she spoke, suggesting that Lydia was a hopeless case.

Lydia ignored the remark and said, 'By the way, Angus Brand will be calling for a prescription for his mother.'

Janice exclaimed boisterously, 'God's on my side where she's concerned. At least she's too old to need my services! Can't stand that woman – all bosom and bracelets. What's wrong with her now?'

'Urticaria.'

'I should have thought her husband was due for that rash,' Janice laughed. 'Have you made out the prescription?'

'Yes, Una has it. She's staying on to give you a hand with surgery.'

Janice frowned, but thought better of rejecting assistance. 'Fine! She can take care of the pests. I haven't your patience. Why she works here when she has her S.R.N beats me.'

'I'm sure she has a very good reason.'

'Giles thought her most attractive… Now I must go and see Mrs Cook. She's home from hospital with her first baby and having trouble with breast-feeding. I'm very worried about her, because she has a dragon of a mother whose help is a form of tyranny… Why do you look at me like that?'

'I was thinking what a strange mixture you are.'

Janice's expression was suddenly sombre. 'Aren't we all?' she said cryptically, as she went from the room.

Lydia was awaiting Noël that evening when Giles appeared at the open front door.

'I wasn't quite sure about these,' he said, holding out the keys of the cottage. His gaze became openly admiring. Lydia looked cool and feminine, in her long white dress, adorned only by a diamond brooch which the rays of the sun struck and turned to flame.

'Oh, keep them until Friday,' she said easily. 'I thought that was understood.'

Giles had acted on an overwhelming impulse to see her; the keys were a lame excuse. In turn, Lydia wondered if he'd hoped to catch Janice before surgery. They gazed at each other with a degree of uncertainty, conscious of emotion building up in the hidden silence, their nearness dangerous, as desire became part of the magic of the fragrant summer evening.

But Noël's voice, calm and confident, broke the spell.

'Ready, Lydia?' He glanced towards Giles, a greeting implied.

Giles tossed the keys a few inches in the air, and then thrust them into his pocket. 'Thanks for letting me keep these,' he said, and walked briskly away.

Noël ignored the incident as he watched Lydia pick up her bag from a nearby chair in the hall. 'We're in good time.' He put a hand lightly on her elbow and guided her out to his car. He looked handsome and commanding, as he took his place beside her in the driving seat, but Lydia was lost to the fact, because her heart was still thudding as she relived those seconds with Giles.

It was typical of Noël that he drove to Stratford-upon-Avon in silence, without in any way suggesting boredom or impoliteness, and it was only when they were settled at the dinner table, their meal ordered, that he said suddenly and disconcertingly, 'Just what are you running away from, Lydia?'

3

Lydia was staggered by Noël's question and echoed, 'Running away! I don't know what you mean.'

'That,' he said convincingly, 'is not true.'

His dogged attitude was a revelation. Until that moment she had regarded him as an isolated personality, whose professional expertise was matched by a fastidious preference for intellectual pursuits, and encyclopaedic knowledge. Yet, here he was, challenging her, probing into her life.

Suddenly, unexpectedly, she relaxed. 'No,' she agreed, 'it isn't true.'

He contemplated her reflectively, ' I'm not talking like the old family friend.' His voice was firm and held a note of warning; but his eyes met hers with gentleness. 'I'm suggesting that the links of the past qualify me to be your confidant, no matter what the problem.'

Lydia sat there with the fragments of her life swirling around her, resolution crumbling in a longing to share at least part of her burden.

'Don't you trust me?'

She hastened, 'Yes; yes of course.'

'Even allowing for your grief over Dennis' death, why have you shut yourself away from life during these past years? Conveyed that your only interest lay in your profession?'

Lydia's shoulders drooped slightly. 'Probably because I was running away from facts. I can't talk about myself, or feel that my affairs, problems, are of any consequence.'

Noël insisted, 'Everything about you is of consequence to me. And I hate that hunted look in your eyes. Sometimes I've even thought it was fear.'

Lydia gasped, 'But it never occurred to me that you'd *notice.*' Her brows puckered. 'Have I been such a bad actress?'

'On the contrary… I merely want to know what role you are playing. Also, why, until now, you've refused to come out with me; made it so obvious that you had no time for my attentions?' He paused before adding, 'Or, for that matter, the attentions of anyone else?'

She did not hesitate as she admitted, 'I don't want involvements, or emotional ties. It is a deliberate strategy.'

'And an impossible one. You know that.

You know it as a woman, and as a doctor.'

Colour rose to her cheeks. The thought of Giles stabbed.

'Tell me,' she rushed on, 'why have you waited until now to question me?'

Noël resisted the impulse to say, 'Because I sense a rival in Giles Palmer,' and instead, replied, 'Because I believe this to be the right moment.'

But still Lydia hesitated, not because of distrust, for she knew Noël to be an honourable man, for whom she had both admiration and respect; yet loyalties were uppermost, and she was not sure that she could reconcile them with her own aching need for understanding.

'Does Timothy come into this?' The question was almost abrupt.

Lydia tensed. 'Why should he?' Her voice was breathless, her expression apprehensive.

Noël didn't pretend. 'Because I've always had reservations about your relationship.'

The comment dismayed and distressed her, and she cried, 'Meaning you don't think I'm a good mother?'

Noël admonished, 'Nothing like that; in fact I cannot really describe my feelings. It's something I *sense* … on reflection, perhaps it would be better if we didn't pursue the matter.'

'No,' she exclaimed with a certain violent protest, as though having marshalled the facts, she was prepared to disclose them. 'There must be something at the back of your mind. I want to know.'

The sudden silence was ominous. Noël looked faintly embarrassed and then resolute. 'Very well–' He met her gaze levelly, 'I'll be honest. I've wondered if your marriage was not as happy as we'd all imagined, and that Timothy might not be Dennis' child.' He rushed on, 'Please believe me, there is no criticism implied in this; only concern and bewilderment.'

Lydia's expression was grave. 'I believe you,' she said, adding with bitter irony, 'but you are so wrong; you see, I am not Timothy's mother.'

Noël gasped, 'You mean he is adopted?'

'It isn't as simple as that.' Her voice faltered and then strengthened as she said tensely, 'Timothy is Dennis' child – by another woman.'

Shock, a degree of anger, made Noël protest, 'Then why in heaven's name are you looking after him?'

Lydia's eyes were suspiciously bright as

she said, 'You could call it compassion, folly, stupidity, or all three, if you like. Dennis was dying when he told me about his infidelity. He was full of guilt, remorse and, above all, of anxiety for the unborn child. He appealed to me… I promised I'd do all I could.' The words tumbled out. 'Now, sitting here with you, capable of rational thought, the story sounds as fantastic as any I've heard during my professional career. And everything in retrospect has a twisted, illusory quality, which tends to invalidate motives… Yet at the time, with drama building up and one's emotions unstable–' She sighed, 'Oh, Noël, I must have been mad to think it would work.'

They didn't speak for a few seconds, and then he said with infinite sympathy, 'You mean that the child is a perpetual reminder of Dennis' betrayal?'

Lydia found it impossible to measure the degree of her own disillusionment, but finally she said, 'Not really. I love Timothy as *Timothy,* but I'm thinking of the fact that, before he was born, his mother agreed to my adopting him and then, afterwards, refused to go through with it, and I was foolish enough to consent to take him, and look after him without that protection.'

'So now you have no legal right where he is concerned?'

'None. I didn't realize the complications of it all. Her circumstances were such that she couldn't take him, and she had to work ... then there was her attitude–' Lydia shook her head sadly, 'I was the *wife* whose help she hated accepting, but needed. Oh, I understood up to a point, but my one concern was Timothy. I'd promised, in effect, to look after him and, by then, I wanted to do so.'

'Now,' Noël said fervently, 'I appreciate why you've always seemed to be walking on egg-shells where he is concerned. You *must* have been mad,' he added grimly, and then, as he saw the hurt in her eyes, added swiftly, 'wonderfully mad. I can't think of any other woman who would have done all this.'

'At this moment,' Lydia admitted, 'I feel anything but wonderful; it is all such a muddle. You suggest that it is impossible for me to live without involvements–' her voice shook, '–even so, what man could possibly tolerate a situation like this – *or* accept Timothy?'

Noël didn't hesitate as he said resolutely, 'I could.'

Lydia gave a little gasp. 'You?'

'I'm in love with you. The possibility has

never occurred to you, has it?'

She looked bewildered. 'No.'

Janice's words, 'He's mad about you', echoed. Just then, Lydia wondered why she had suddenly confided in Noël, and realised that meeting Giles had awakened emotions responsible for her present impetuosity. In consequence, she had automatically lowered her defences and become a human being, aching for understanding, instead of an automaton, disciplined to resist both pain and happiness, except in bleak moments of recollection. Timothy represented a solace for love's betrayal, and she wept for him because she was powerless to safeguard his future; she could give him only security for the moment, while his mother reaped a subtle revenge as a palliative for her own resentment and jealousy.

'We could see this through together,' Noël urged.

'No, Noël,' she whispered, her voice heavy with regret. 'God forbid that I should marry for Timothy's sake. That wouldn't protect him, in any case, should his mother want him back.'

'Which is a kind way of telling me what I suppose I know already – that you do not love me.'

She said wistfully, 'I'm not sure I'm capable of loving now. Suffering dulls the senses after a while.'

'So does celibacy,' he retorted crisply.

Her voice was urgent. 'I don't want any more conflict, confusion, doubt. I have enough problems already.'

'Now you are manipulating–'

She interrupted him, 'I'm trying to be honest. It's true that I don't love you in the way you mean, but your moral support, your companionship, represents a very great deal. It would be very easy to cheat in the circumstances.'

He looked at her searchingly, 'If you really wanted my support, you would convince yourself that you were justified in marrying me. Love has been known to grow out of affection and friendship.'

Lydia did not attempt to argue.

'Now,' he said reflectively, 'I understand why you sold your house and left Tetbury so soon after Dennis' death. At the time I thought it a hasty decision, but it was not for me to interfere. Death changes so many things.'

Lydia said tensely, 'It was convenient to move to London and stay with Janice who was then working at Southlane Hospital.

My part-time locum job … well, I gave it up when Dennis was taken ill. It had served a good purpose, seeing that Dennis was away a great deal. Engineers have that privilege,' she added ironically, memories crowding back. 'I couldn't confide in anyone, and was glad in some ways that our parents were dead. It would have been difficult to put on an act for them, or to explain the circumstances.'

Noël nodded. 'What was Janice's attitude towards your decision over Timothy?'

Lydia looked solemn. 'She had no patience whatsoever with me. The only word in her vocabulary was "termination". That was out of the question in any case; the pregnancy was too far advanced. What I had foolishly regarded as an adoption case became a nightmare when adoption was flatly refused. I could do nothing, and if I'd had any sense I'd have opted out then.' She tried to keep control as she added, 'But, you see, the mother didn't *want* the child. God knows what would have happened had I not looked after him.'

Noël's expression was grave, 'I wonder she agreed originally to his being the posthumous child and, by implication, yours.'

Lydia nodded, 'I, too, was baffled by that.

But it was her idea and very simple to execute. I'd been out of this district long enough actually to have had Timothy. With hindsight, of course, I realize that it was a clever manoeuvre on her part, completely to involve me, without giving me any legal rights. Timothy is still her child; registered in her name.'

'So you are doubly vulnerable.'

'Yes,' Lydia said heavily, 'a fact of which Janice reminds me on occasion.'

'That does not surprise me,' Noël retorted, never having really liked Janice.

Lydia hastened, 'I shouldn't have said that … all the same, it stresses my vulnerability. I've no one to blame but myself. My only excuse is that I was so emotionally overwrought after Dennis' death that I was blind to the dangers, and allowed myself to be *led* once I'd initially agreed to help. I couldn't confide in anyone, and at one point I felt that for Timothy to be acknowledged as Dennis' son, seemed the most honest way out of the situation. My adopting him, in addition, would have tied up all the loose ends and been so simple.' She added bitterly, 'I didn't expect bad faith, despite the treachery of the past. I was so naïve. Everything was being done in the mother's interests and with her co-operation. But, of course, it had all been carefully planned. I served a purpose. She'd never had any intention of letting me adopt Timothy.' Lydia stopped, shocked by her own anger, while feeling that she ought not to have confided in Noël, and dragged up the past which only emphasized her abysmal folly. Folly. Yet had caring for Timothy, loving and protecting him, been that? But for her, where might he be now? With a reluctant mother, part of a one-parent loveless family.

Noël tried to be optimistic, 'Is the adoption really so important? Timothy is your son to everyone who knows you; there is no question of doubt, or curiosity.'

Lydia said gravely, 'He hasn't mine, or his father's *name*. How about when he needs legal identification? Prior's Gate, also, is his home only just so long as it serves his mother's purpose to keep him there. As you said yourself, I've no legal rights. Once I'd adopted him, he would have been safe; she could never have taken him away.' Lydia looked infinitely sad. 'And I should have been able to tell him he was adopted, so that there would never have been any need for secrecy.'

Noël exclaimed half-apologetically, 'Mine

was a short-sighted remark!' He asked abruptly, 'Is his mother likely to be married?'

'I wouldn't know. Why?'

'Because, in that event, she might be more co-operative.'

There was no hope in Lydia's voice as she said, 'Jealousy is always destructive. I have a feeling that she is waiting for the moment when she can do the most harm, and that she'll strike when it hurts me, and Timothy, most.'

'Equally,' Noël suggested, 'she may never strike at all.'

Lydia met his gaze. 'True; that is where the hell of suspense comes in.'

'I see what you mean. Even so, you can fight.'

Determination flashed into Lydia's eyes, 'Oh, yes; I can fight, but revenge is a deadly weapon and I have Timothy's happiness to consider... I'm sorry, Noël. I'm spoiling the evening. I'd no intention of ever telling you the truth.' She looked confused and bewildered.

'I value your confidence and your trust,' he said quietly. 'I shall not refer to the subject again, but you know where to come if you want to talk – at any time... May I just say how touched I am by your love for Timothy;

your concern for him. In the circumstances, it is nothing less than noble. No, don't contradict me… And if we don't hurry we'll never get to the theatre.'

Lydia's eyes glistened as she murmured, 'Thank you for understanding.'

Noël was only just beginning to grasp the enormity of the problem and wished that, in Janice, Lydia had greater moral support. He said irrelevantly, 'Why did you and Janice go into partnership?'

Lydia answered without hesitation, 'Because when Uncle died it seemed a sensible thing to do. Janice was tired of hospital life, and I wanted to continue my career. I deluded myself that, although our temperaments had always clashed, the professional bond would enable us to find common ground and build up a worthwhile practice. Also, she was family, and I felt that would be good for Timothy.'

'And is it?'

'Up to a point, yes. She can be very good with him when she chooses.' Lydia paused. She was going to add, 'although she is critical of everything connected with him, and of me, generally', but felt that to be disloyal, and hurried on, 'but the relationship isn't all I'd hope for.'

'Perhaps Dr Palmer will be a good influence... I'm surprised you didn't choose an older man.' Jealousy prompted the utterance.

'I should not have had Janice's co-operation in that case, and since we've to work together... I'm tired of fighting, Noël.'

They looked at each other in silence.

Lydia remembered little of the rest of the evening. She was in no mood for Shakespeare, and had she not known *As You Like It* backwards, would have found it unintelligible, since her concentration was nil. Normally the atmosphere of the theatre entranced her; on this occasion memories washed over her, bringing the past to life, prising open old wounds, highlighting fear, and when, finally, Noël drove back to Prior's Gate, he said with consideration, 'I'm not going to invite myself in for a coffee.'

She raised her gaze to his. 'Thank you for the evening, Noël. I'm sorry I spoilt the mood with my self-indulgence.'

'I'm not sorry,' he said bluntly. 'At least I know what I'm fighting. I want to marry you, so don't lose sight of that fact... Good night, Lydia.'

'Good night,' she murmured, knowing that he would wait, and watch, until she was actually in the house. The idea that he wanted to marry her was disconcerting, and a complication from which she instinctively shrank. She had never for a moment seen him in a romantic light, and realized that nothing could ever be quite the same between them in the future. Perhaps, when it came to it, she had regarded everyone as cardboard figures, pigeonholed for no better reason than that she was dead to emotion; incapable of being roused. Giles slid insidiously into her thoughts, mocking her self-assessment, and when she reached her bedroom she stood at the open window looking out on the moonlit scene, her gaze turned in the direction of the cottage. Soon he would be living there, and she felt his presence as though some part of his personality lingered to haunt her.

Giles' advent at Prior's Gate proved to be an unqualified success. Patients liked him, and colleagues respected his ability and sterling qualities. As summer gave way to the mellowness of autumn, Lydia experienced an overwhelming relief because the intervening months had passed without friction, Janice having been both reasonable and co-operative. They worked as a team and neither jealousy, not malice, marred the general harmony.

'Now,' Janice said to Lydia one evening when the day's work was done, 'don't you think I was right in wanting Giles to join us, instead of some old dodderer? You must admit he's a great asset, and that the practice is thriving.'

'You were more than right. These have been happy months.'

'You're certainly more human,' Janice said bluntly.

Lydia laughed, 'Probably because you've been more agreeable and less aggressive!'

Janice's smile was inscrutable. 'Proving, maybe, that the leopard can change its spots.'

In turn, Giles had been wary during that time, aware that to establish a healthy professional relationship with two women required tact and neutrality. Even so, after three months both Lydia and Janice remained a mystery to him. Janice's *bonhomie* was not what he had expected, while Lydia's apparent relaxed acceptance of him was faintly baffling. Their initial sensual rapport might have been frozen by a friendly sexless collaboration, which Giles somehow distrusted. Nevertheless he had been grateful to be spared emotional conflicts, and congratulated himself on his control, particularly in moments when it would have been simple to ignore discretion.

It was after surgery one evening when Lydia arrived unexpectedly at the cottage, asking if he would accompany her to see a patient who had all the symptoms of appendicitis.

'I'm uneasy, Giles,' she said urgently. 'This has blown up suddenly. Mark Stubbs is a stoic who would never complain unnecessarily. Neither would Nita, his wife, be agitated for no reason. I'd like your opinion.'

'Of course.' He grabbed his medical bag and went out to the car with her. 'I looked after Mark Stubbs when he had 'flu... Wife's Dutch and most attractive.'

Lydia laughed. 'I agree.' She added, 'Timothy and their daughter, Faith, go to nursery school together. We're all friendly acquaintances... If this should be an emergency, we'll get him into Hill House. You'd operate.' She was thinking aloud. 'They like you, and that's half the battle.'

'Suppose we wait until we see what we're up against,' Giles suggested. 'Or does your women's intuition tell you that–?'

'My woman's intuition tells me that it's

fatal to plan a quiet evening, hoping to watch a special television programme! One invariably ends up like this – trying not to break the speed limit.'

'The hazards of general practice.'

'How true.' She turned off the Tewkesbury–Ledbury road into the drive of the Stubbs' secluded house.

Lydia's fears had been well founded, for after examining Mark Stubbs both she and Giles knew that they were dealing with an explosive peritonitis, and that there was no time to lose. Lydia alerted the nursing home, arranged for an ambulance, and a short while later the patient was on the operating table. Lydia attended at Nita's request. When finally Giles tore off his rubber gloves he exclaimed, 'Hell, that was a near thing!'

Theatre Sister nodded. She liked Giles and appreciated his skill. Not all surgeons, she reflected, had Giles' finesse.

Lydia smiled, the tension was over. 'I'll go and tell Nita,' she murmured, and made her way into the waiting room where Nita was sitting, white-faced, shaken.

'All's well,' Lydia said jubilantly, keeping her fingers crossed as she spoke. Post-operative complications were an ever-present risk.

'Oh, thank God!' Nita was choked, her eyes tear-filled.

Lydia admonished, 'You ought to have sent for me first thing this morning.'

'Mark didn't want to bother you … just because he had a bit of a pain and vomited … he thought it was something he'd eaten.'

Lydia shook her head and despaired. Self-diagnosis invariably led to an emergency. 'Now,' she said gently, 'you go home; Mark will be out for quite a while, and you need some rest.'

Giles joined them, his quiet reassuring manner both attractive and impressive.

Nita said in her fascinating, faintly broken English, 'I don't know what I should have done without you both.' She added breathlessly, fear returning, 'He will be all right?'

'Of course,' Giles promised.

Later, out in the smoky mist of the September night, Giles looked at Lydia and said, 'I think a brandy and something to eat is in order, don't you? How about the Hop Pole?'

'But I–'

He cut in through what he knew was to be her refusal and insisted, 'The Hop Pole. I've a soft spot for the place.'

'Very well.'

During the past few months Lydia had become a consummate actress, managing to treat Giles with friendly detachment, giving an impression that while she liked and respected him, there was no question of his appealing to her other than as an associate and future partner. She had, in fact, been amazed by her own sang-froid, almost as though, after the initial emotional shock of their meeting, she had completely regained her composure and thrust him out of her thoughts. By adroit manoeuvring she had avoided all social contacts that didn't include Janice, or Noël, or both. Thus she had been cushioned against danger. Now, as they went into the familiar cocktail bar, she was immediately aware of him as a person, divorced from work. It was an exciting, yet disturbing, sensation.

'I'd prefer a sandwich to a meal,' she said hastily, as he was about to book a table.

He shared the preference.

'It seems yesterday and, contradictorily, a decade since we were last here,' he said, when they had been served. 'Mark Stubbs' misfortune is my gain. Do you realize that this is the first time we've been out together since I joined you?'

Lydia forced a laugh. 'You make the fact

sound like a grievance. Is there any particular reason why we *should* have been out together?'

'Only the desire to do so.' He spoke deliberately and looked straight into her eyes.

Lydia's heart-beat quickened; she lowered her gaze, conscious of his nearness and a surge of emotion that made her shiver. He looked strong, tenacious and immovable, as though defying her to resist him.

'It was a busy summer,' she said evasively, sipping her brandy, and afraid that her hand would shake.

'In which you have become more of an enigma.' He persisted in sustaining the personal note.

'I think,' she said smoothly, 'that we have an excellent understanding. The word "enigma" doesn't come into it.' She followed that with a reference to a patient and the validity of a particular diagnosis.

Giles studied her with unnerving intensity. 'The fear has come back,' he said.

She immediately thought of Noël. He had talked of fear, and both he and Giles were right. She feared commitment in the circumstances, yet was unable to play a light-hearted role when challenged by a conversation involving herself.

'You seem intent on making complicated judgements.'

He shook his head in denial. 'I'm trying to find the real *you,* Lydia. Oh, I know the pleasant detached colleague of the past few months, but she doesn't tie up with the Lydia who sat in that same chair beside me the night you told me you wanted me in the practice. *She* was enchantingly elusive, but there was a promise in her smile as though giving a concession to fate. Now, you're all tensed up, resisting everything I say. Not *daring* to relax.'

Lydia protested, 'You wouldn't have studied psychiatry by any chance? Honestly, Giles, you seem determined to – to–' she faltered.

'To – what?' His voice was commanding.

'To make an issue of our relationship.' Her eyes flashed as she spoke; a flame of anger spurted, lit by panic.

He held her gaze as he said with disarming gentleness, 'So you admit that we *have* a relationship?'

'We could hardly work together otherwise,' she managed to say, trying to curb emotion.

'I wasn't thinking of work.'

Lydia's heart was thudding as she sat there, lost to everything but the power and mesmeric attraction of the man beside her. She lowered her gaze and then raised it to his, '*I* was, Giles.'

He said with conviction, 'Sooner or later you will have to stop running away from life.'

Lydia looked bewildered and defeated. First Noël, now Giles. She gave a thin little laugh and exclaimed, 'You really have some quaint notions about me.'

'That rather depends on what you mean by "quaint",' he retorted.

At that moment Noël detached himself from a small group at the far end of the cocktail bar and walked towards them. His gaze went from face to face, registering disapproval as he said, 'I certainly didn't expect to find *you* here.'

'Is there a law against it?' Giles asked tersely, getting to his feet.

Lydia explained the circumstances, realizing that by so doing she appeared to be justifying the tête-à-tête.

Noël sat down beside her, his attitude proprietory. Actually he had telephoned Prior's Gate and Janice had told him about Mark Stubbs, suggesting that he, Noël, would most likely find Lydia with Giles at the Hop Pole, provided their professional commitment allowed.

Giles fumed inwardly. Noël's presence struck a discordant note, and shattered his hopes of drawing Lydia back into an atmosphere of emotional awareness. Giles recognized Noël's ability and professional skill, and their relationship maintained a surface harmony, while beset by mutual jealousy and distrust whenever Lydia was involved. It was as though in that moment Noël had thrown down the gauntlet and wiped out the uneasy truce.

'What,' Lydia hastened, 'are you doing here?' She looked questioningly at Noël as she spoke, feeling that she was suddenly under a microscope. 'I thought you were having dinner with the Morrisons.'

Why, Giles thought unreasonably, should Lydia be concerned about what Noël was doing that evening? And why did she seem so agitated?

'I was, and I have.' Noël sipped the brandy he had brought with him to the table. 'Unfortunately Grace's mother was taken ill. Grace had to drop everything and leave for Bath. Philip went with her. From all accounts I'm afraid it was a coronary.'

Lydia looked dismayed. She liked Philip and Grace Morrison, and had met Grace's mother, Gillian Swayne – a vital, attractive woman in her early fifties. 'I'm sorry,' she said.

Noël sighed and then indicated Lydia's glass. 'Can I get you–?'

'No; no thank you,' she hastened. 'A drink and a sandwich has been our supper.'

Noël glanced at Giles. 'And you?'

Giles declined another brandy and said to Lydia, 'Time we were going … don't you think?'

Lydia looked flustered. The remark emphasized what Giles had made obvious: that Noël was intruding.

But Noël said smoothly, addressing Lydia, 'By the way, I've discovered a restaurant you'd like – Gorse Lawn, on the Ledbury road. I thought we might try it sometime next week.' There was a note of confidence in his voice, and an automatic assumption that she would fall in with his suggestion. He finished his drink. 'I'll look in before surgery tomorrow morning.'

Lydia stood up, murmuring something inarticulate. She felt uncomfortable. Noël's attitude was possessive, almost as though their relationship was of an intimate, rather than a friendly, nature, and she realized that it was for Giles' benefit. Annoyance built up as the three of them walked through to the hotel entrance.

'We came in my car,' she said crisply as they reached the street. 'Good night, Noël.'

'Good night.'

'Talk about a watch dog,' Giles said, as Lydia drove off.

'Don't be ridiculous.' She forced a laugh, emotion building up out of tension and frustration.

'Will you have dinner with *me* next week? Or has Noël the monopoly?' There was an aggressive note in Giles' voice.

Lydia protested. 'Of course not … I'd love to have dinner … thank you.'

They reached the cottage in a matter of minutes. The car stopped abruptly and silence fell. Lydia was acutely conscious of Giles' nearness, and of the excitement quickening her heart-beat. Almost without realizing it, she slid out of the driving seat, thus escaping from any physical contact.

'A coffee? Brandy?' Giles suggested, moving to her side.

'No, thank you.' She adroitly stepped back, pulling the car door towards her and shutting it as she settled again in her seat. 'I don't know why I got out in the first place,' she muttered.

Giles rested his elbow on the frame of the open window and looked down at her.

'Running away again,' he said coolly. 'But I warn you, you won't get far.'

She quipped, 'And I haven't far to go!' With that, trembling, she thrust in the gear. But in that second their eyes met and the look he gave her was so passionate, so intense, that he might have leaned forward and kissed her. No word was spoken, and she drove away trance-like, afraid to face the truth: that she loved him, and had done so almost from that first moment of meeting.

4

Lydia hadn't any time to dwell on her own problems the following morning. Surgery was heavy and the waiting room bulged. Chest complaints; menstrual and menopausal troubles; a fractured patella and, said Janice at the end of the session, 'Uncle Tom Cobley and all!' She flopped down in an armchair in the common room, adding as Giles joined them, and addressing Lydia, 'Did your boy friend find you last night? I thought I shouldn't be far out if I told him you might be at the Hop Pole.'

Giles answered, 'We *were* at the Hop Pole; and the boy friend *did* join us!'

Janice crossed the room to the telephone as it rang.

'Speaking … Mr Templeton!' Her voice was instantly alert. 'Bleeding … I'll come at once.' She replaced the receiver. 'I said Madge Templeton would never go to term with this fifth pregnancy. And I don't like it… Giles, would you come along? We may have to get her into hospital – operate.

Anyway, I'd like your opinion.'

Giles glanced anxiously at his watch. 'I'll have to keep Mrs Crawford waiting.' He glanced hopefully at Lydia, who said, 'Don't worry; I'll have a word with her, she's very understanding.'

Una appeared with coffee. Janice snatched a cup from the tray, took a sip, made a face because it was too hot, and handed it back.

'A Mr Bates telephoned during surgery,' Una told Lydia. 'Trevor Bates. He will ring again later.'

Lydia and Janice exchanged surprised glances. *'Trevor!'* Lydia cried in a breath.

'The past catching up,' Janice suggested, then, with Giles, hurried away.

Una stood, still holding the tray, waiting for Lydia to take her coffee, but Lydia seemed transfixed.

'Dr Vane! *Coffee!*'

Lydia apologized. 'How busy are we today?' she asked, absentmindedly stirring her sugarless drink.

'Pretty hectic; and there's Mr Jenkins coming to tell you what's wrong with him, and how badly he's been treated, while keeping any symptoms a dead secret!'

Lydia felt stressed and impatient. 'Why pick on me? Why not Dr Palmer?'

'He doesn't like Dr Palmer.' Una chuckled. 'Dr Palmer sees through him.'

'And he deludes himself that I don't?'

'Exactly.'

'Then I think I'll suggest some X-rays and a few tests,' Lydia announced wryly. 'That will cure Mr Jenkins of his imaginary ills ... but we mustn't grumble; he provides a little light relief.'

Una laughed, and having studied Lydia carefully said solemnly, 'I *wish* you'd see a doctor.'

At that Lydia laughed outright. The idea was ludicrous.

'I'm serious,' Una persisted. 'Oh, on the surface you appear to be all right, but you're exhausted and overworked.'

'I also look ninety! Go on, cheer me up!' Lydia added, 'Has anyone else noticed my declining health?'

'Nanny for one.'

Lydia looked amazed.

'She thinks so highly of you, Dr Vane. We all do.'

'Then you must all be sickening for something,' Lydia commented banteringly, trying not to dwell on the reappearance of Trevor from the Tetbury days. 'Now, have a look at that day sheet of yours... Madge Templeton,' she murmured irrelevantly, wondering what possible reason Janice had for enlisting Giles' help. It was highly unlikely that his services would be needed.

Giles was voicing the same sentiment as Janice drove swiftly to the outskirts of Bredon where the Templetons had a rambling old Manor house.

'My motives were psychological. Madge Templeton holds the erroneous subconscious belief that I've been unsympathetic towards this pregnancy, when I've merely been very concerned. Her blood pressure's too high; she's never been strong, and with four children and a fifth on the way … well! She'll be relieved to see you.'

'But I don't know her.'

'That's not the point. Your presence will cut through her phobias… I'm being proved right, you see. I suggested sterilization after the last child… Well, here we are.'

A distracted, ashen-faced husband flung open the front door.

'She's collapsed … doesn't *know* me…'

Madge Templeton was dead; her heart had not been able to withstand the shock of a miscarriage. Janice never forgot the expression on Ralph Templeton's face when he realized the fact; neither would she forget the four motherless children huddled in a pathetic whimpering group by the open nursery door.

Later, back in the car, Janice sat stunned, tears running down her cheeks.

Giles put out his hand and clasped hers, touched by her reactions.

'Thank goodness Nurse Brown is available,' she murmured. 'I must get her over here immediately, and keep an eye on the husband. At least his mother is on her way from London.'

Giles slumped in his seat. 'It doesn't bear thinking about.'

'It ought not to have happened!' Janice cried; 'but a doctor cannot *force* a patient to take advice. Those children–' Her voice cracked.

No further comment was made on the short journey back to Prior's Gate, but Giles felt that he had seen a hitherto unknown facet of Janice's character which enhanced his opinion of her.

Lydia was standing at the front door with Timothy and Nanny as Giles and Janice went into the hall on their return.

'I'm going on my pony,' Timothy said with delight. He looked up at Lydia, then at Nanny, and finally to Giles and Janice, giving them all a beaming smile, looking back over his shoulder as Nanny led him away.

'Madge Templeton?' Lydia asked anxiously.

Janice told her what had happened.

'Oh, no!' Lydia cried, and again, *'No.'* She added shakenly, 'They were so *happy.*'

Instantly Janice's mood changed, her voice harsh, 'Haven't you seen enough to know that tragedy always strikes people who are happy? The gods must be jealous – jealous,' she added bitterly. 'I'm going to get Nurse Brown and run her over there. I telephoned from the house. Tell Una I'll be as quick as I can.' With that she hurried away.

Giles watched her and surprised Lydia by saying, 'This has upset Janice more than I'd have believed possible. Somehow I've never imagined her being so involved... Goes to show how little we know one another.'

Lydia's heart seemed to stop beating for a second, and then thud on in fear as she saw the expression on Giles' face. She experienced all the pain of love as she looked at him, realizing that even his appreciation of Janice hurt her, while also recognizing that any display of jealousy would endanger the entire structure of their professional life.

'Did you hear what I said?' Giles added,

'You look – strange.'

'Sad,' she hastened. 'A doctor's life is always poised on the edge of tragedy.'

'For once we agree... Now I must see Mrs Crawford.' His almost brusque attitude softened as he said, 'Don't forget about our dinner date. I leave you to choose the evening.'

'Next Wednesday?'

'Splendid. I must find somewhere that Noël has never heard of – if that's possible.' He turned back as he reached the corridor leading to the practice quarters, 'I'm wondering who Mr Trevor Bates may be. Someone from the past could mean anything.'

Lydia did not want to think of Trevor. He brought back memories she had endeavoured to stifle. In addition, Timothy had not been born in those Tetbury days... Wednesday ... her thoughts swirled around like leaves in autumn. She loved Giles and, without conceit, felt that he was, to some extent, attracted to her. Why not tell him the truth? Of course the situation was complicated, but if he should love her in return, would he not accept Timothy, and the disadvantages? The possibility raised her spirits. Why be a defeatist? Why prejudge her own case and build up obstacles merely because of an instinctive fear of rejection? Heartened, she went back to her consulting room, ready to face a formidable list of patients.

It was at supper that evening that Janice said, 'Trevor rang while you were out on the Langton case. He's coming for drinks on Sunday morning.'

'Oh!'

'You don't sound too keen.' Janice's smile was faintly taunting.

'I was wondering what he was doing here, seeing that he originally intended staying in South Africa for good.'

'Well, now he's *home* for good! And settling in Kineton.'

'Really.'

'Apparently his father died and left him a great deal of money.'

'Oh!' Lydia said again.

'You haven't seen him since Dennis died,' Janice said pointedly.

Lydia looked at Janice very levelly, 'Neither have you. He was far more your friend than mine.'

Janice made no comment for a second, but her voice was firm as she exclaimed, 'He and Dennis were pretty close. Trevor will be surprised to know you have a son ... his wife's dead, by the way.'

'Irene!' Lydia was shocked.

'She died of leukaemia a year ago. I always felt that you had a soft spot for Trevor.'

Lydia gasped, outraged, 'You *know* that's not true. *You* were the one who–'

Janice's eyes were slits in a mask-like face. 'And *you* know how absurd *that* is.'

Lydia tensed. She dreaded losing the comparative peace of the past months. 'Suppose we don't hold any post-mortems? I shall be happy to see Trevor again. Let's leave it at that.'

Janice smirked, finishing her wine, 'I thought you might like a third string to your bow. With old faithful, Noël; plus an obvious crush on Giles, why not rope in Trevor too? You've always thrived on numbers and conquests.'

There was an electric silence which Lydia broke by saying curtly, 'Hadn't you better go over to see Ralph Templeton?'

Janice glared. 'I'll go when I'm ready, and not before. I hope he's satisfied with his brood of kids. The person I'm sorry for is his mother – having to cope with them. If you ask me, Madge is well out of it.'

'Janice!' There was near-horror in Lydia's voice. 'I thought you were genuinely upset by her death … or was that just an act to impress Giles?'

'Go to hell!' Janice retorted, flinging down her table napkin and, flouncing out of the dining room, walked blindly into Noël who was crossing the hall. '*You* here again,' she snapped.

'And what was all that in aid of?' Noël asked, as Lydia appeared.

Lydia sighed and shook her head.

'I wondered if you'd come out and have a drink with me,' Noël suggested lamely.

'I don't feel like going out, but you stay and have a brandy and coffee with me.'

It was what he had hoped for, and accepted with alacrity, then jerked his head in the direction of the front door as Janice slammed it. 'The honeymoon over?' he asked wryly.

'Something like that.'

'There's no antidote for the green-eyed monster,' Noël said with emphasis.

Lydia ridiculed the possibility of jealousy, crying, 'That's absurd!'

'And you are absurdly naïve in some ways,' he pointed out.

'Possibly.' She twisted her wedding ring in a little nervous gesture. 'I wish I had more confidence, Noël. Oh, not professionally;

I've overcome my original fear in that direction, but in other ways–' Her large thoughtful eyes sought his reassurance.

'After hurt and disillusionment, insecurity is almost inevitable.' He stopped and then hurried on, not wanting to highlight the past, 'Anyway, if you ask me, Janice wants Giles' attention, knowing that it is already directed towards you.' And although Noël spoke lightly, he was studying Lydia's expression intently, aware of the colour dyeing her cheeks. 'I *thought* you'd understand,' he added.

Lydia didn't want to understand, or to accept his observation as truth. 'I understand that even the things that seem obvious where Janice is concerned, are invariably misleading.'

'Not on this occasion,' Noël insisted. 'I'm just warning you.'

Coffee was brought and Lydia asked Noël to pour out the brandy. He did so with the ease of a man completely at home and in command. And as they lifted their respective glasses, Noël said urgently, 'Marry me, Lydia.'

Panic returned as she averted her gaze. Her love for Giles seemed tangible and impossible to conceal, but she managed to say, 'My feelings for you haven't changed, and I can't pretend.'

'I don't ask you to change, or pretend... I've allowed the months to go by without bringing the subject up–'

'I realize that,' she interrupted, 'and I've been glad. I've even known some degree of peace.'

'Giles' advent has certainly appeared to work miracles. The calm before the storm, perhaps. I take it nothing has altered where Timothy is concerned?'

'Nothing,' Lydia said dully. She cried, 'Oh, Noël, I don't want to *think* about it.'

'An escapist attitude won't solve anything,' he suggested firmly.

'Neither would marriage for the wrong reason.'

'But it wouldn't *be* for the wrong reason,' he reminded her.

How, she asked herself, could she tell him that Giles was the only man with whom she could share her life?

'It is not enough to *be* loved, Noël; one must love in return ... don't you see?'

He didn't answer her question, merely sat there looking at her very steadily, as he said, 'All the same, the day will come when you will be glad for me to take care of you. Love does not automatically solve problems; more often than not, it creates them.'

Lydia felt a breath of fear. His voice was that of authority, his words seeming prophetic. She recognized a truth that she would hate to be without Noël, and having confided in him, he seemed doubly important, because she was completely relaxed in his company, or had been until that moment. Her love for Giles set her apart, while contradictorily giving life a new dimension. She did not comment on Noël's observation, but said swiftly, 'I'm a fatalist, Noël. Time answers all our questions … and that brings me, somewhat irrelevantly, to the fact that Trevor Bates is back in the district.'

'Bates,' Noël said somewhat disparagingly. 'I thought he had gone to South Africa for good.'

Lydia explained the circumstances and that Irene, his wife, had died of leukaemia.

Noël frowned. He had not known Trevor well, but had always distrusted him, and been surprised that Dennis had encouraged his friendship.

'He's coming for drinks on Sunday morning. Join us.' Lydia made up her mind to invite Giles, also.

'Very well.' Noël was aware of Lydia's air

of distraction; of an expression in her eyes which isolated him. He added briefly, 'I think you'd prefer to be alone now.'

She looked at him in slight bewilderment, finding it difficult to dissemble. He got to his feet.

'I'll talk to you when we have dinner together next week … how about Wednesday?'

She told him that she was dining with Giles, and suggested Friday.

He agreed, his manner frigid. When he left, she had a momentary feeling of guilt, until she reminded herself that Noël had no proprietory claim upon her, and that she had not encouraged him to foster any such belief… Should she telephone Giles? Sunday was a valid reason.

He answered her ring almost immediately, the sound of his voice had the effect of an electric shock, quickening her heart-beat and making her tremble.

'Lydia!' He uttered her name with obvious pleasure, and then added swiftly, 'Trouble?'

'No … I wondered if you could come for drinks on Sunday morning?'

There was a slight pause before he replied, 'As a matter of fact, Janice has already invited me. She called in on her way to the

Templetons. I'd love to come.'

'Oh, good.' Lydia heard herself saying the words as though she were an actress who had carefully rehearsed them. She felt slightly sick, for while she appreciated that Janice had every right to take the initiative, she could not help distrusting her motive, particularly in view of all that Noël had said. Yet suppose Janice should be attracted to Giles – in love with him. What then?

There was an awkward pause before Giles asked, 'Is something wrong?'

Lydia exclaimed swiftly, 'No ... I was just looking out; it's a heavenly night ... the harvest moon.'

'I'm beginning to appreciate autumn – the countryside. After London it's a completely new world. We ought to be walking by the river.' His voice was low and husky, creating an exciting intimacy.

'Perhaps next Wednesday,' she suggested.

'I'll hold you to that.'

When she replaced the receiver, Lydia asked herself if Giles was all things to all people; conveying far more than he actually felt, and flirting with words rather than kisses. Or was she really as naïve as Noël had hinted? The possibility seemed ludicrous. Nevertheless, when it came to experience she had very little other than imagination upon which to draw, since she had never indulged in sensual escapades, or considered affairs a proof of sophistication.

Janice returned a little later, poured out a brandy, and said truculently, 'Ralph Templeton's mother looks like a shovelful of death; Nurse Brown can't stay because she has an imminent midder, and the whole place is like a morgue. What can *I* do?' She didn't expect an answer and went on, 'With four children, he won't find it easy to get anyone to marry him in a hurry.'

Lydia said quietly, 'Let him bury his first wife before you think in terms of a second.'

Janice made an impatient sound. 'Anyway, I don't want to go on as their doctor. You'd better take over. I'm sure he wouldn't have any objection – probably be grateful. I'm not his favourite person, nor he mine.'

'Very well, if that's how you feel. I'll talk to him a little later on.'

'You're so good with children,' Janice exclaimed with a touch of sarcasm. 'I don't profess to be. Heaven knows why I chose obstetrics. Not really my scene.'

'What is?' Lydia spoke with a patient desperation.

'Having a good time; being free to do as I

please, and with whom. I'm sick of this professional straitjacket. I notice that the strictly professional relationship doesn't wash any more so far as Giles is concerned. Fine. Suits me.' She finished her brandy. 'Good night.'

Lydia remained trance-like in her chair. Whichever way she turned she felt that her life had been punctuated with mistakes and faulty judgements; now she was paying for them.

Janice's mood had completely changed the following morning. She joined Lydia at breakfast, blithe, smiling, suggesting that they made Sunday morning open house. 'We haven't done any entertaining for ages. Trevor's bound to know some of the people around here, anyway.' She added enthusiastically, 'We'll invite Jane, Una and Dulcie. Jane can bring Paul … for a husband, he's quite fun. Una and Dulcie can bring their respective boy friends.' She stopped. 'Dulcie may not even have a boy friend; she's quite pathetic over Noël. Sad! He doesn't even know she's alive!... Anyone you particularly want to ask? Giles is coming, by the way.'

Lydia ignored that, and said, 'Unfortunately Mark's in hospital, so that rules him out, and Nina, too. The Bensons are away–' Lydia paused. 'I can't think beyond our patients, and leave it to you.'

'Very well.'

Janice finished a hearty breakfast and then went along to Jane's office. Una appeared from Reception, which led from the common room.

'Ah!' Janice beamed and told them about Sunday. Neither could accept the invitation because of genuine previous engagements.

'Never mind,' Janice said, unperturbed because she had thought the whole thing up for no better reason than she knew Lydia disliked such gatherings. 'Another time. Pity. Dr Palmer is coming.'

'Pity indeed!' Jane grimaced. 'He's special.'

Janice looked from face to face, her expression smug and self-satisfied. 'I agree... Just between ourselves – in fact, *strictly* between ourselves – I intend to marry him. That way, we'll not only keep him in the family, but in the practice!' With those words she smiled knowingly and left them.

Una gasped, 'She wasn't *joking!*'

'That cookie,' Jane retorted, 'never jokes; and if she were to do so, the joke would never be on *her* ... we'd better fasten our seat belts, we're in for a bumpy ride.'

‘I was thinking of Dr Lydia,’ Una said quietly.

‘So was I,’ Jane agreed.

5

Trevor Bates felt uneasy as he drove to Tewkesbury that Sunday morning. On reflection, he considered it a mistake to have contacted Lydia and Janice now that he was settled in Kineton. Far better to have allowed the past to bury its ghosts. Nevertheless, as his car stopped at Prior's Gate and he saw Janice appear at the front door, his heart quickened its beat. She had not lost her compelling insolent charm as she greeted him.

'I always told you we should meet again,' she said, her eyes bright and provocative.

'It was ungallant of me to have contradicted you.'

She thought swiftly that he hadn't changed, and while he was not distinguished, he had the scrubbed appearance of the athlete, plus the indolent air of a playboy, and was equally good in both roles.

'I agree … you haven't lost that gorgeous tan since your return,' she exclaimed, her gaze disturbing. 'Come and meet the family.'

'"Family"?' he echoed.

Lydia and Timothy stood hand-in-hand in the hall.

Trevor looked at them, surprised, almost shocked.

Timothy announced, after taking stock, 'Mummy says you won't know me … I'm Timothy; I was born after my daddy died.'

Trevor felt a pang as he said hurriedly, 'Hello, Timothy,' and added, 'Lydia, how *are* you?'

'Are you a doctor?' Timothy asked. 'They're all doctors here, 'cept me and Nanny.'

'No; I'm not a doctor.'

'Oh.' Timothy gave him an endearing smile, and said with quaint resignation, 'I'm going to find Nanny, and then my friend Alan is coming. He *can* stay to lunch, Mummy, can't he?'

'Of course, darling.'

Janice admonished, 'And don't make too much noise.'

Timothy flashed her an old-fashioned glance. 'You're always *cross,*' he said bluntly, and ran up the stairs.

Trevor smiled. 'He's a fine little chap.'

Lydia caught at her breath. 'I'm so sorry about Irene.'

He nodded. 'Bad business ... I'd no *idea* about Timothy. How proud Dennis would have been.' He stopped, embarrassed.

'Let's join the others and have a drink.' Janice was impatient.

Noël had met Trevor briefly in the old days, while Giles regarded him with faint suspicion, unashamedly wanting to preserve the *status quo* at Prior's Gate. He noticed that Lydia was faintly ill-at-ease, while Janice took command, conveying that she and Trevor had previously enjoyed a free-and-easy friendship of no particular significance. He also noticed that Lydia diverted the conversation whenever nostalgia crept in, reluctant, or even afraid, to talk about the past. This struck him as suspicious, since Trevor had been an acknowledged friend of Dennis'. Even when Timothy was mentioned, Lydia seemed unwilling to discuss him, glossing over the questions asked. Giles was also aware of the way in which Noël butted in to change the subject when Lydia showed signs of anxiety. They might have been in league to keep a secret. Yet what secret?

Giles asked, rather abruptly, 'What made you return to England, Mr Bates – leave behind all that sun?'

'A good question,' Trevor responded easily. 'Many reasons, I suppose. Friends mainly. I'd lost touch with most of them – it happens without intent, really.' He indicated Lydia and Janice. 'But one picks up the threads as though there had never been a gap... I can't get over Timothy...'

At that second the sound of laughter from the nursery above punctuated his words. Trevor smiled. 'Brings a house to life,' he added unexpectedly.

Janice flashed him a surprised, even startled, look.

He said jerkily and involuntary, 'Irene was pregnant when she died.' He emptied his whisky glass and rushed on before anyone could comment, 'Returning to your question, Dr Palmer, I rather think that fact influenced my decision to return home; and was perhaps my subconscious reason for doing so. Escape ... yes, I'd like another, Janice.' He handed her his glass.

It was a strange gathering. Lydia felt that she was standing apart, watching, listening, in isolation. Trevor revived the past; tore open old wounds; emphasized her present precarious position, and her impotence where Timothy was concerned. A fierce protective instinct welled within her as Trevor said, on leaving, 'I'll come again, Lydia, if only to see that son of yours … say goodbye to him for me.'

'I's here,' came a lisping voice from the top of the stairs. 'Will you help me fly my kite when you come again?'

'I certainly will… Goodbye, old chap!'

''Bye.'

Janice walked out to the car with Trevor.

'I'll come over,' she said in an undertone.

He looked at her, startled.

Lydia joined them. 'It's been good to see you,' she said sincerely.

'I'm glad I'm back…' He got into the car and drove away.

'Out of character for Trevor to take notice of a child,' Janice exclaimed, almost resentfully.

Lydia's voice was quiet as she commented, 'He would have made a good father… Irene's death seems doubly tragic–'

'Because she was pregnant,' Janice cut in. 'About time you gave up your illusions about having children … you sure are a devil for punishment.' Her laughter grated.

Lydia winced; depression overwhelming her.

Noël and Giles remained in the sitting room, each wanting the other to leave first.

Giles had done his routine hospital visits and, as far as was possible to judge, had the rest of the day free.

'Why not stay to lunch?' Lydia suggested, looking at them in turn.

'You *know* that I'm going to see my sister,' Noël protested. There was a suggestion of annoyance because Lydia had forgotten. 'Why on earth she and her husband went to live at Great Malvern, beats me. They won't stay there.'

Lydia forced a laugh. 'Arden was always unpredictable. I ought to have telephoned her. Tell her I'll do so this evening. Oh, and she'd be interested to hear that Trevor's back. They always got on well together.'

Noël gave a grunt, then as he was about to leave, said, 'I'll look in for a drink after supper.'

Janice waited until he had actually gone, before saying significantly, addressing Giles, 'You'll notice how very much at home Noël is here.' She turned to Lydia, 'when are you going to marry him?'

The sudden silence was embarrassing. Giles hung on Lydia's reply.

But Lydia ignored the question, and asked Giles coolly if he had decided about staying to lunch. Her heart sank as he made some flimsy excuse, his voice cold, his manner withdrawn. Janice accompanied him from the house.

In a moment of utter misery Lydia covered her face with her hands, fighting to prevent the tears. She didn't see, or hear, Timothy come into the room. His voice was plaintive, 'Mummy … are you *crying?*'

Immediately she dropped her hands and managed to laugh, but Timothy clung to her as he persisted, 'I don't want you to cry–' The words were thin and choked as he added, 'Not *ever.*'

Lydia got to her feet, picking him up as she did so. 'Not ever,' she promised. 'And when you've had your walk I'll read to you before tea.'

He bobbed up and down excitedly. Then, 'Alan's gone home with his nanny,' he explained in his quick, childish fashion. 'His grandpa and grandma are coming to see him … why haven't *I* a grandpa and grandma, Mummy?' His brows puckered, his expression sad, 'I's *no* one–' The large round blue eyes were tear-filled. 'Not even a sister or brother or–'

Lydia's heart ached. 'You have me, darling.'

'But you're a mummy – you *had* me.

ust fit her in.'

Lydia agreed, and Una left them. An awkward silence fell, which Lydia broke by saying, 'About Wednesday–'

Giles didn't hesitate – anticipating that she was going to cancel their dinner date. 'Don't worry; I understand perfectly.'

'But–' Lydia looked confused. She had only wanted to alter the time because she had a late appointment. Obviously Giles was grateful to escape taking her out.

'Far better leave it at that,' he said with quiet finality.

Noël joined them at that moment. Giles put down his coffee-cup, nodded, and left.

'The X-rays of Mrs Owen,' Noël began, then stopped. 'Is anything wrong?'

She protested impatiently, 'Of course not.' She wanted to cry; to give way to the pain crushing her heart. 'Don't fuss, Noël. I'm not a patient.' She added quickly, and as lightly as possible, 'By the way, if you'd prefer we went out to dinner on Wednesday this week, I'd like to do so.'

Noël looked both pleased and surprised, but was wise enough not to mention Giles, or question her as to why the previous arrangement had been cancelled.

'Fine,' he exclaimed. 'Wednesday is

That's different.' He thought for a second. 'I've got Aunt Janice … don't like her much. No, I *don't*.' He was emphatic.

Nanny appeared in the doorway, her usually bright, rosy-cheeked face, anxious.

'Talk about quicksilver,' she said to Lydia.

'What's "quicksilver"?' Timothy lisped slightly.

'I'll tell you later on,' Lydia promised.

He sighed, shook his head, and baffled, exclaimed, 'Why is it always "later on"?'

At that moment Giles was saying to Janice, 'Were you serious just now when you spoke of Lydia marrying Noël?'

Janice replied casually, 'Of course. Hadn't you guessed?' As she saw his shocked expression, she hurried on, 'Oh, they're not officially engaged – obviously.' Her pause was significant. 'I doubt if they ever will be; it's not that kind of relationship … I just happen to think it's *time* they married. Anyway, it's a long story.'

Giles had never felt more depressed.

'Would I be right in believing that there's some mystery attached to it all?'

Janice lowered her gaze. 'I didn't say so.'

'You didn't have to.'

'The trouble is that Lydia runs in all directions at once. But Noël is the cornerstone of her life. God knows what she would do without him. But it's not for me to tell them how to conduct their affairs. I just happen to like *tidy* relationships.'

'So do I,' Giles agreed, and there was a sad finality in the utterance.

'Are you doing anything special this evening?' She spoke innocently.

'No.' He paused. 'Why?'

She made a little helpless gesture. 'I was wondering if I might come in for a drink – to avoid playing gooseberry when Noël returns.'

'Very well.' There was no enthusiasm in his voice. 'We could go to Broadway and have a meal.'

'I'd like that,' she said eagerly.

One fact upset Giles more than all others as he reflected on the events of the morning: that when challenged by Janice about marrying Noël, Lydia had remained silent. He wished now that he had pursued it, but what difference would it have made? *'Lydia runs in all directions at once.'* The words struck a painfully familiar chord, and left him in no doubt where he stood. All he could do in future was to maintain a purely professional relationship.

Lydia sensed the subtle change in Giles'

manner the following morning whe[n]
took surgery. Afterwards, as they wer[e]
the common room, he said, struggli[ng]
sound impersonal, 'Straightforward
for me this morning ... how about you

'So-so.' She tried to keep her voice
shaking, and to avoid his eyes. 'There's
patient I'd like you to see for me.'

He found it impossible not to be move[d]
the appealing gentleness of her expressi[on]

'Of course.'

'It's Mrs Brecon; she's lost a lot of wei[ght]
and there's a mass in her abdomen; a
she's been having a good deal of pain –
quite a time, too.'

Giles said with sympathy, 'And it's no u[se]
asking why she didn't come to us befor[e]
God knows I understand a patient's fears.'

'She hasn't even told her husband tha[t]
she's been to see me... I've arranged wit[h]
Noël for barium tests tomorrow at ten. I'[d]
like you to see her before then.'

'I'll juggle the appointments. How abou[t]
nine-thirty?'

'Thank you.'

Una brought the coffee as usual, saying
Lydia, 'Dr Hunt has to go to Mrs Glenmc
who wasn't due for a fortnight ... if y
could see her ten-fifteen patient? You c

excellent for me… Now, going back to Mrs Owen and the cervical spondylosis, there's a C6 root lesion and–' He cursed as the telephone rang on the private line.

Lydia answered it, and Janice said, 'I'll be here for quite a while. Is Giles there?'

'No,' Lydia replied abruptly. 'Can I–?'

'I'll speak to him later. 'Bye.'

Lydia was shaking; she felt empty, her nerves jangling. But she feigned concentration, thankful when Noël hurried away to what he termed 'a scared-stiff patient'.

Lydia found herself listening for Giles' voice at the end of the day. Would he come into her room, as was customary, or would he go to Janice? This was the lull before surgery, and the house seemed as empty as a school when the children were on holiday.

But her door opened and Giles said smoothly, 'I'm giving Janice a hand with surgery this evening… I understand Noël is taking you out to dinner… Ah, Noël–' Giles stood aside as Noël reached the doorway, then, looking at Lydia, added, 'I won't forget Mrs Brecon at nine-thirty tomorrow morning… Pleasant evening.'

Lydia, puzzled, turned to Noël when they were alone, 'Giles said you were taking me out to dinner. It hasn't even been mentioned.'

Noël spoke with authority. 'It was a snap decision… Let *them* do the work. You're tired out.'

Lydia hadn't the will, or the strength, to argue.

'And I'm taking you *home* for a meal,' he said firmly. 'Mrs Digby knows.'

Lydia smiled for the first time. 'Mrs Digby is special – a wonderful housekeeper … you haven't to worry about a thing, and her cooking is marvellous, too.'

'Which means that you could leave everything to her, and continue your career once we were married.' He spoke confidently.

Noël's house, overlooking the river, had the simplicity of a Scandinavian dwelling, and for the first time Lydia viewed it with assessment. To marry Noël, and create a home for Timothy. His pathetic words about not having any relatives hurt her. He was old for his years, and had an uncanny perception, instinctive in children. Yet how could she plan for him when she had no permanent jurisdiction over his future? Equally, how could she drift, merely because of that fact?

'I like the sense of space here; the uncluttered look without starkness,' she said involuntarily.

Noël smiled. 'I'm delighted that you notice after all these years! I've always thought of it as a shell out of which you could create a home to your own liking.'

Again Lydia had a suffocating sensation of panic, as the thought of Giles overwhelmed her.

To her surprise Noël put his arms around her, and looked down at her with a solemn intensity as he said gravely, 'Together we can fight whatever lies ahead so far as Timothy is concerned. I shan't weaken your position.' His voice deepened, 'But I cannot go on like this much longer. If you will not marry me, I shall leave here altogether – go right away.'

His words shocked her because she knew he was serious – a man of strength and decisiveness. And what was she? she asked herself. A woman who had clung to a dream like some love-sick adolescent; building up a look, a few words, into some great romance with a man who, doubtless, had pretended far more than he actually felt.

She moved away from Noël with a degree of finality.

'Give me a month,' she said quietly. 'I

must try again to resolve things concerning Timothy.'

'Very well,' he agreed; 'a month.' His expression was uncompromising.

It was a week later when Janice, on her free day, announced that she was going shopping in Cheltenham, and would probably make a friendly call on one or two patients in the area. 'Catch up,' she said, 'on those "do look in for a drink" offers, which we hardly ever take any notice of.'

Lydia felt immediately expansive: it would be a relief not to have to contend with Janice's unpredictable moods.

'A good idea... Are you looking for anything special to buy?'

'A long skirt or two.' She added, 'Tell Mrs Lane that I shan't be in for any meals, but ask her to leave me some fresh orange juice in the fridge. Oh, yes, and get her to tell that husband of hers to clean out the garage. It's filthy. I don't know what we pay them for! They've their own quarters, everything found, television–' She stopped, abashed by Lydia's steady gaze.

'They've also been here for twenty years.'

'What's that got to do with it?'

'Everything. We can concentrate wholly on our work; be fed, and never have to worry about a thing – domestically. They're irreplaceable in these days, and you know it. I'll mention the orange juice, but as for the garage!' Lydia made an impatient sound, 'Not only is it clean, but our respective cars are clean, too.' Lydia escaped to her consulting room, her nerves taut.

Janice cursed herself for being difficult for no better reason than that she had been scared lest anything should prevent her getting away; also that it always gave her malicious pleasure to provoke Lydia.

Giles caught up with her as she was leaving the house.

'I'm off shopping,' she said blithely.

'So you told me last night... The shops are not open all the evening.'

Janice grinned. 'I'll see if you are in when I get back.'

'I shall be in,' he assured her.

She waved him an airy goodbye and shot down the drive.

Once out of the district, she drove straight to Tetbury.

Trevor received her with misgiving. He had no illusions about Janice, but was still attracted to her, having tried to deceive himself to the contrary.

Janice glanced around her, appreciating

the old-world garden, and black-and-white timbered cottage which looked picturesque enough to grace the pages of *Country Life*. Emotion stabbed sharply, and she touched the edge of suffering as she met Trevor's wary gaze. His greeting was formal, his attitude withdrawn. She uttered banalities about the surroundings, enthusing as they went into the spacious hall with its antique furniture and rich oak panelling.

'This is quite perfect,' she said in a breath.

'I bought it as it stood,' he explained. 'The owner was suddenly whisked off to America on a permanent assignment. Money certainly simplifies life. I was able to take over the staff – modest staff. A couple – the Bryants – after the style of your Lanes; plus a daily. Works well.' He added, 'Particularly as they have their own quarters over by the orchard. The previous owner had lived abroad before, and knew the value of not having staff under one's feet. They benefit too … drink?'

Janice was almost feeling unwelcome. 'Please; dry martini.'

'With gin?'

'So you haven't forgotten?'

'That you like gin? No. But I've noticed that there's a great deal of martini drunk these days, without gin.' He turned her question into a subject for comment, rather than nostalgia. 'I suppose the price has something to do with it.'

'Quite possibly.' She took the glass. Would he invite her for lunch? It was impossible to tell what he was thinking, or feeling. 'What do you do with yourself all day?'

'I ride; hunt – play golf. Time doesn't drag, I assure you... No need to ask what *you* do.' He added deliberately, 'Have you patients to see in the district?'

'No; I came to see you.' The words rushed out because she no longer felt in command of the situation.

He was immediately aware of her, and of the desire in her eyes. His pulse quickened.

'I don't know if that is a good idea,' he managed to say.

'Then suppose we let time decide...' She sighed and settled in her chair. 'I can't quite believe that you are here. I'd reconciled myself to never seeing you again.'

'I thought you'd be married.' He spoke bluntly.

'And now that I'm not?' Her voice was low.

'Suppose we have lunch somewhere?' he hastened. 'The Bryants are not on duty today and I know of a delightful place at Badmington.'

Janice had regained a little of her lost confidence. 'I'm not very interested in sitting at a table and eating. I want to catch up on the news – hear all about you, and your plans.'

'Having lunch doesn't prevent our talking, and you know all the news. South Africa; Irene's death; my return.' He tried to sound matter of fact.

Janice held his gaze. 'And your feelings? Did you ever think of me?'

'Of course I thought about you.' There was impatience in his voice.

'And now that we're here together?'

'Damn you Janice; I still want you,' he said roughly, and on a note of exasperation.

'And I, you,' she whispered as she got to her feet, and the next minute was in his arms.

An hour later as she lay beside him, passion spent, all the tension, the frustration, drained away. She watched the curtains fluttering at the bedroom windows, with luxurious content. After a while, she raised herself on one elbow and looked down at him, admiring his nut-brown body.

'The past few years have been hell for me,' she said reflectively. 'Work, responsibility –

Lydia. And no one suspecting how I missed you, or what we'd been to each other.' An almost savage, primitive note crept into her voice. 'I don't have to pretend with you; basically, we're two of a kind... Why do you frown? It's true, or we shouldn't be here now. And you're free. Before–'

He stirred uneasily, not wanting to be reminded of Irene, or his infidelity.

'Don't drag the past into it, or deceive yourself,' he said gruffly. 'There's no question of our ever marrying.' He resented his own weakness in having made love to her. He didn't want strings, or complications.

Janice winced, but countered, 'I'm not asking you to marry me. I've other plans in that direction.'

'Giles Palmer.'

'Quite possibly.'

'You'd be at each other's throats in a week,' Trevor scoffed.

'Not with you in the background to excite me, darling. I need excitement – anything to deaden the monotony.'

Trevor sat bolt upright in the bed. 'Oh, no; you're not going to involve me in anything like that,' he insisted sharply.

She smoothed her cheek against his shoulder. 'It won't be a question of "involving" you,' she whispered. 'We've never been able to resist each other.'

He looked at her, his expression changing from impatience to reawakened desire.

'No,' he admitted grudgingly, 'that hasn't changed.' As he spoke, he drew her back into his arms.

Later, they awakened with a start as Janice cried, 'What time is it?'

He looked drowsily at his watch. 'Three o'clock! That damned dog barking!'

'Yours?'

'No; the farm nearby… That was a lovely sleep.' He smiled at her. 'We've missed lunch.'

'Who cares about lunch?' she said airily, and then disappeared into the adjoining bathroom, turning on the bath taps and calling out, 'How about some coffee?'

'Good idea.'

She reappeared and they stared at each other, realizing how naturally they had slipped back into intimacy without effort, or strain.

While they were drinking their coffee, Trevor congratulated himself on having made his position perfectly clear, so that they both knew where they stood. At the moment he had no intention of becoming entangled in any new association, therefore his relationship with Janice would not jeopardize his position in any way.

'Lydia was pleased to see you,' Janice said irrelevantly.

'And I, her.' He added, 'Timothy's a bright little chap – quite touching, the way he spoke of his father. Dennis would have been proud of him.' Trevor studied Janice with sudden concern. 'It must have been a grim time for you all. I heard of Dennis' death from a casual acquaintance who happened to be in Cape Town on holiday.' Trevor paused, then, faintly puzzled, added, 'Lydia left Tetbury very quickly, but I suppose it was for the best.'

Janice sipped her coffee. 'That's debatable. I had the flat in London, which made it simple.'

Memories lay between them and he said involuntarily, 'I was never sure if Irene knew about us.'

Janice shrugged her shoulders. 'Women are pretty intuitive and don't miss much … you didn't want a divorce, anyway.'

'No,' he agreed. 'I didn't want a divorce, or to cause you a hell of a lot of trouble. I'm glad I made the decision to clear out.'

'And to come back,' she prompted.

'Yes; in spite of myself.'

'Come over to Prior's Gate whenever you feel like it. No complications likely there. We can be perfectly natural together. Hell,' she cried, 'I'd like a place on my own! I envy you this, with only yourself to think about.'

'That, doubtless, will pall in time.'

'And until it does, we'll live for today… It's all been perfect.'

He didn't attempt to deny the fact, or to understand it.

As they said goodbye, she murmured, 'I'll come again as soon as I can – when the Bryants are not on duty, of course. I'll telephone first.'

She drove away, feeling at one with the world. The sterile years vanished from memory. Everything with Trevor was right. They were sexually harmonious, and on the same wavelength emotionally. How would she feel if he were to marry again? The question disturbed her, and she dismissed it, concentrating on her own affairs. Once married to Giles she would be secure, and Trevor would represent the icing on the cake. Every woman, she argued, should have a lover as well as a husband, in the same way that most men had mistresses. Equality of the sexes. But why Trevor? Why was it that his touch roused her as no other man's had ever done? With diplomacy and discretion, she could preserve that halcyon state while protecting her career, and building up the charade of married life. A self-satisfied expression curled her lips. And there was nothing Lydia could do about it.

6

Giles went into Lydia's consulting room that afternoon, having come straight from operating on Mrs Brecon.

'You were right,' he said quietly. 'Stomach *and* liver. There was nothing we could do.' His sigh was full of regret as he made a helpless gesture, adding, glad of the brighter news, 'But the ovarian cyst biopsy on Paula Morgan is benign.' His expression softened, 'Janice was very concerned about her; she's been very helpful.'

Lydia nodded. She could not bring herself to enthuse about Janice. 'I'm dreadfully sorry about Mrs Brecon. It's so ironical; her husband has just retired, and they'd made so many plans.'

Giles exclaimed with feeling, 'I've noticed that plans seldom work out. Life is very much a day-to-day assignment.'

'Which is a good philosophy if one wishes to avoid commitments.'

He looked astounded, amazed at her ability to discount her own involvements, and wanting openly to challenge her about Noël. Yet what right had he to do so? And he certainly could not betray Janice's confidence.

'Surely that is better than having commitments and pretending otherwise,' he countered.

She stared at him, baffled. 'Meaning?'

He shook his head and the words were wrenched from him. 'That you are a magnificent dissembler, Lydia.' He hurried on, 'I take it you will be going to see Mrs Brecon later on? There's the question of what to tell her.'

Lydia struggled to concentrate on the case, shocked by Giles' previous remark.

'At this stage she will be satisfied to have had the operation. She has very little medical knowledge; neither has her husband.'

'Then we must play it by ear. I'll have a word with Sister Hawkins.'

'Mr Brecon will want to see you as soon as possible.'

'I know.' Giles' sigh was full of compassion. 'Amazing how much these cases upset us, despite all our training. It's damnably hard when patients *want* to know the truth, and even worse when one has to keep it from them; but I suppose when we reach the Brecons' age we shall be looking forward to many more years of life.'

Lydia lowered her gaze; her voice broke as she replied, 'Depending on how happy we are.'

They looked at each other with uncertainty, emotion silencing them. Giles was about to speak when the telephone rang. It was Una, saying that his patient had arrived.

Lydia visited Mrs Brecon that evening, and on her return to Prior's Gate, drove towards the cottage. If she needed an excuse to see Giles, she argued, the patient provided it. All she knew was that she couldn't stand the present strained atmosphere, the tension, between them. His words, *magnificent dissembler,* haunted her, and she was determined to find out exactly what he meant. It was impossible to sustain any conversation at Prior's Gate, with the telephone ringing at the wrong moment. But as she slowed down, and turned into the lane, she saw that Janice's car was parked at the cottage gate. A wave of hopelessness and desolation swept over her as she accelerated. She might have known that Janice would be there, and that, in all probability, the whole day had been carefully planned.

At that moment Giles was saying to

Janice, 'Reverting to our conversation that Sunday, when you mentioned Noël and Lydia–' His brows puckered; there was an expression of doubt and anxiety in his eyes.

'You mean, their being lovers?' Janice spoke in a matter-of-fact tone, adding swiftly, 'I took it for granted you'd already guessed ... I wasn't *criticizing* them, so much as wishing they'd get married and have done with it.'

'And the mystery?' Giles prompted. 'I know there's something – something I've sensed, but cannot fathom. Lydia's attitude – a certain anxiety in the way she avoids discussing the past.'

Janice sighed wearily, 'I also avoid talking about it, because I hate disloyalty. And yet it lies like a shadow even over *our* friendship,' she said deliberately, 'because you don't know where you stand.'

'That is certainly true,' he admitted, still baffled, but finding it distasteful to be discussing Lydia so objectively.

'And now I have to weigh up what's best for *us.* I don't want things to be spoilt.' Her words were soft and insinuating. 'We've become so close recently, and understand each other better.' She moved her chair and walked a few paces up and down the room, worry wrinkling her brows. 'On the other hand, I want you to make allowances for Lydia.'

'Good heavens,' he protested, 'that doesn't come into it! I'm not here to sit in judgement. Anyway, facts seldom tell the whole story. As I see it, the question of trust matters most. I just want to *understand.*'

Janice sat down again, aware of his resistance and defensive manner, as he stood with his back to the chimney-piece.

'I agree, only I'm in a difficult position.'

'Why?' He was instantly alert, almost challenging.

'Because I haven't known quite what to do… Now I'm going to tell you the truth – in confidence. I shall endanger Lydia's position far more by my silence. Inevitably suspicion leads to conjecture and investigation. Unfortunately, Lydia's life has been a chapter of mistakes, or whatever word you prefer.'

Giles tensed, half wishing he hadn't begun the questioning.

'In what way?' He spoke fearfully.

'Dennis was about to divorce her, but he died before the proceedings had been started,' Janice said quietly.

'What!' Giles' voice rose in disbelief.

'You see, Lydia's grief was for the loss of her lover who conveniently returned to his wife the moment Lydia was widowed. She had no love for Dennis; his death was a relief.'

Giles listened, speechless, remembering conversations with Lydia when he first joined the practice; her remarks when they had dinner at the Hop Pole about not perpetuating unhappiness by dwelling upon it. In retrospect, her attitude had not been consistent with the sadness of a woman still suffering from the loss of her husband.

Janice went on gently, 'She was in an invidious position, Giles. I often wonder how she came through it all. Timothy was not Dennis' child, but her lover's. I'm the only person in the world who knows that.' Giles gave an incredulous gasp as Janice went on coolly, 'I was never sure whether the lover knew of her pregnancy. Lydia's pride might well have prevented her telling him. Had Dennis not died, God knows what would have happened. As it was, Timothy became Dennis's posthumous child.'

Giles looked, and felt, stunned. Lydia's thoughtful sad eyes haunted him. So this was the explanation, and the end of the mystery.

'And the man … who was the man?' He spoke fearfully.

'I can't tell you that. It wouldn't be fair. As far as I know, he is no longer in the picture.' Janice paused. 'Now do you understand why I'm so concerned about her *marrying* Noël? Why I want her to have a stable future? Not just for her sake, but for Timothy's.'

'I understand,' Giles murmured, feeling suddenly bereaved. 'Does Noël know all this?'

'I believe so.'

'Then why *doesn't* she marry him?'

Janice hesitated, 'I've always had the subconscious feeling that she still clings to the forlorn hope that Timothy's father may one day return to her… Oh, I know how fantastic it seems, but she wouldn't be the first woman to delude herself.'

'But that's ridiculous,' Giles protested vigorously, amazed by his own resistance to the possibility.

'Love can *be* ridiculous,' Janice said simply.

Giles had no answer. He felt empty and deflated. There had been something almost ethereal about Lydia, a depth and delicacy which this story confounded.

'I ought not to have told you!' Janice cried, looking agitated. 'I didn't intend to, only I knew you were curious, and even a few harmless questions, asked at the wrong time, could precipitate a crisis.'

Giles did not emphasize how near he had come to asking such questions.

'I've wanted to avoid any further upheaval,' Janice went on quietly. 'I couldn't have stood it.' She paused for effect. 'Lydia came to me when she left Tetbury. I had a flat in London and a hospital job which I enjoyed. I never wanted to go into partnership with her – never! But she needed my moral support, and what else could I do? I was *family,* and created an air of respectability. Oh, I admit that I'm often beastly to her ... it's just that I feel trapped.' She looked pathetic and dejected as she added, 'I'm not really hard, or cynical... Oh, Giles, your coming here has transformed my life. To be able to talk like this; be honest about the past, knowing I can trust you absolutely – you can't imagine what a relief it is.'

Giles merely nodded, looking bewildered.

'If Lydia messes up her life again,' Janice said fiercely, 'I shan't raise a finger to help her. What I'd really like is to get right away. Perhaps, when it comes to it, I have a selfish, ulterior motive for wanting her to marry Noël. Then I should feel free – released from a self-imposed responsibility.'

'What *I* can't understand,' Giles protested, 'is the secrecy about her relationship with Noël – irrespective of whether she's going to marry him or not. I nearly asked her about it earlier today, when she talked as though she hadn't commitments of any kind.'

Janice managed to keep her voice free from the alarm she felt, 'For goodness' sake, don't start questioning her! You'll never get a straight answer, and she always looks so innocent! That's what infuriates me most of all.'

Giles frowned, shrinking from the truth, and reluctant to accept it.

'And you won't think less of me for confiding in you?' Janice was disturbed by the resistant expression on Giles' face. His attitude confounded her preconceived ideas.

'I'm grateful to have been put in the picture,' he said. 'Just one question: Does Trevor Bates come into the story?'

Janice gave a little gasp. 'Trevor? Good heavens, no! What gave you that idea?'

'Something in her manner that Sunday –

an uneasiness.'

Janice pointed out with telling emphasis, 'You've overlooked the fact that Trevor used to live in Tetbury, and has now returned there.'

Giles persisted, 'Did he know the man in question?'

'Oh, yes; quite well.' Janice rushed on, 'You *will* stay in the practice?' Even as she spoke, she felt the question to be indiscreet and irrelevant.

Giles averted his gaze, his emotions chaotic. 'Suppose we leave that for the time being.' He added, anxious to avoid further discussion, 'I think we need a drink.'

Janice waited until she had the glass in her hand before pleading, 'Don't judge Lydia too harshly. She adored that man.'

Giles took a gulp of his brandy. 'I'm thinking of all she must have suffered.' He spoke gently and with compassion, then, glancing at his watch, added restlessly, 'Let's go out and have something to eat.'

Janice stiffened, curbing her annoyance because of his reactions, having hoped for a lengthy post-mortem. A few minutes later she got up from her chair and went close to him, her hand shyly touching his. 'Thank you,' she murmured.

'What for?'

'Being you.' She raised herself on tiptoe and lightly kissed his cheek.

Involuntarily, the following morning, Lydia found herself saying to Giles, 'Why did you call me a "magnificent dissembler" yesterday?'

Giles studied her with incredulity, amazed that she could ask the question when she knew how apt the description was, but not wanting argument or dissention, fell back on a vague, 'My mood, probably; or our being at cross-purposes. We're on much safer ground talking shop – which brings me to Mrs Brecon! I know we agreed to play the case by ear, but when it actually comes to seeing her husband today–' He shook his head to convey helplessness.

Lydia felt that she had been dismissed; that what she had previously regarded as a close relationship, had been reduced to a professional exercise. There was nothing more she could say; no further questions she could ask. She controlled her voice as she suggested, 'You could imply that the operation was rather more serious than you thought, and that further tests had to be made.' She faltered, and then rushed on, 'Once he realizes that she will not need a further operation, he'll go along blindly for a while.'

But Giles had completely lost concentration, as Janice's words re-echoed, *'Dennis was going to divorce her, but he died before the proceedings could be started'!*

'Giles!' Lydia's voice seemed to reach him from a great distance. He apologized, struggling to collect his thoughts, saying, 'You're right; in moments of crisis, nature allows people to believe what they want to believe... What did you think of Mrs Cook?'

'I agree with hospitalization – complete rest and a rigid diet are essential for a duodenal ulcer, no matter how much she protests.'

The conversation continued entirely along professional lines, and when Giles left, Lydia thought they might have been two people at a bus stop discussing the weather. She couldn't have said that he was curt, or even unfriendly, but something in his manner made him a stranger. As against that, was she building it all up? Was it in her mind, her love for him cutting through sanity? But as another fortnight passed and his attitude did not change, the former excitement and anticipation vanished, leaving only heartache and desolation.

It was after surgery one evening when Giles said, as he was about to leave, 'Oh, Lydia, are you doing anything special this coming Sunday?'

For a second she held her breath, an expectant happiness touching her, as she answered, 'No – why?'

'It's just,' he explained somewhat hesitantly, 'that if you could be on call from about midday … I want to take Janice to meet my aunt. She lives in Ledbury, as you know.' He watched Lydia intently, but her expression was inscrutable.

'Of course; no problem.' Her voice was smooth.

'Thanks. Let's hope there are no emergencies. Autumn can be dicy.'

'Yes … I've promised Timothy a reading session.'

Giles wished he could hear Timothy's name without it having significance.

'Splendid,' he said jerkily. 'He'll love that.'

Walking to the cottage, Giles asked himself if she would ever have told him the truth about the past. But why dwell on that? What did it matter with whom she had been in love? Or what her relationship with Noël was now? Oddly enough, she didn't appear to have been seeing as much of Noël lately.

Giles quickened his pace, knowing it was useless denying that Lydia had attracted him, and that he had deluded himself the attraction was mutual. He put his key in the cottage door and slammed it behind him. The sitting room looked bleak and seemed cold, despite the central heating. For some inexplicable reason, he felt a stranger there. And why was he taking Janice to meet his aunt? Questions, he thought with disgust, but never any authentic answers. He had joined the Vane practice with ambitious hopes, and found the past months both rewarding and stimulating. Then why allow the facts concerning Lydia's past to affect his attitude, or his future? He was not the custodian of her morals. He poured himself a small whisky and sat down, resting his forearms on his knees, looking down into the glass as though seeking inspiration. Snatches of conversation drummed in his brain. *'Why did you call me a magnificent dissembler?' 'Timothy was not Dennis' child, but her lover's.'* A pang shot through him as he realized how fond he had become of the child; a fondness of which, until now, he'd been only vaguely aware. Timothy's bright, intelligent face took shape in the soft light; his amusing and pertinent questions echoing, making Giles feel protective. He finished his drink and wandered into the dining room where a cold meal awaited him – left by his much appreciated daily – but he made a grimace, having no appetite. The telephone rang and he answered it abruptly.

Lydia said, 'I've got to go out to see the Gilliat girl … would you take the calls? If you have to go out, Mrs Lane will be here.'

'Gladly,' he said, meaning it. 'What's Janice doing?'

'Having dinner with the Bretts… You knew; I was there when she told you.'

'Of course … I remember now.'

'Sorry to bother you: good night.' The line went dead.

Giles ambled into the kitchen, made himself some instant coffee in the largest beaker he could find, and took a cold sausage from the fridge, which he ate in his fingers as he returned to the sitting room. The coffee tasted foul and he put it aside in disgust. The telephone rang again, sounding as loud as a fire alarm. This time he answered it almost with relief.

'Mrs Horton … your husband … chest pains. No; don't give him anything. I'll be with you in a matter of minutes.'

Giles grabbed his medical bag and went

out into the frosty night air, breathing deeply. The Hunter's Moon lit up the countryside, etching the reflections of every tree. He raced away. Nothing like work to take one's mind of one's own problems. What did he know about Mr Horton? Ah! Fussy type; over-dramatized everything. Probably flatulence.

It was.

Mrs Horton, an agitated anxious woman, who would have loved a more adventurous life, apologized for dragging Giles out. He felt sorry for her, and set her mind at rest by assuring her that he preferred to be 'dragged out' for nothing rather than not to be sent for when urgently needed.

'My husband gets so worried about himself – so nervous, Dr Palmer.'

Giles smiled wryly. 'You give him that bicarbonate… Goodnight.'

'I will. Thank you again.'

Giles drove past Prior's Gate on his way back. Only the front door lights were visible through the screen of trees, otherwise the house was in darkness. Obviously, Lydia was still out. It struck him that she worked far too hard, but he thrust aside the thought, and let himself into the cottage with quiet resolution. The silent emptiness remained.

Janice said to Lydia the following morning, 'Thanks for agreeing to be on call this Sunday, Giles and I appreciate it.'

Lydia made a suitable comment, adding, 'You seem very pleased with life.'

'I am... Who was it said that "love makes us wondrous kind"?'

'Love?' Lydia held her breath, knowing that there was one aspect of the present situation she dare not face.

'You must have noticed.'

'I've noticed your being very much more pleasant to me,' Lydia said, determined not to put any words into Janice's mouth.

'That's what I mean about love! I feel generous to everyone. Miracles do happen, after all. It began with the Templeton case. Giles began to see me in a different light.' She smiled. 'At one time I rather thought he preferred *you* to me.' Janice gave a little laugh. 'Which only goes to show how wrong one can be.'

'Meaning?' Lydia's mouth was dry; a sick sensation made her cold.

'That while he hasn't exactly put it into words, I know he is in love with me.' Janice's voice sharpened. 'Don't tell me that you haven't sensed a change in him, or noticed how much time we spend together.'

'I hadn't jumped to any conclusions.' Lydia felt that her heart was beating in her throat, stifling her.

'Well, I'm confiding in you... We *are* sisters, and you come into it, after all.'

'Yes,' Lydia said on a note of authority, 'I come into it.'

'I hope you're not jealous.'

The knife went deep as Lydia shrank from the truth.

'Don't be foolish. It's time you made up your mind about the future.'

Janice scoffed, 'Look who's talking! What about you and Noël?'

Lydia's expression changed, and there was a note of sternness in her voice as she countered, 'I resent your insinuations about Noël.'

'They're not insinuations! I'm sick of being asked when you and he are going to be married.' Janice paused, and then went on gently, 'You've been pretty uptight lately; people have noticed that, too. They're not blind, Lydia.'

Problems, responsibilities, overwhelmed Lydia in that moment. She had tried not to think about Noël's ultimatum, but the month was nearly up. During the intervening weeks he had been almost reserved, seeing her less than usual, thus emphasizing the fact that he had no intention of putting her under pressure.

'I'm really concerned about you,' Janice went on, 'concerned about your future.'

Lydia stared at her aghast. 'Don't be a hypocrite, Janice.'

'Of course, if you're going to twist everything I say… But you know that our lives are bound up together, and our respective future husbands are part of the pattern. We could make a cosy little foursome. You can't deny *that!* I'm quite certain that Giles will ask me to marry him, so I'm not fantasizing. The set-up would be ideal.'

Suddenly Lydia's love for Giles became fiercely protective. 'Are you sincere about your feelings for him?'

Janice looked completely convincing. 'Absolutely sincere. I suppose the attraction was there from the beginning, when I was so persistent about his joining us.' She saw Lydia start, and a shadow cross her face, then rushed on beguilingly, 'I'd never hoped to feel like this, and as for marriage! Well! *You* understand how I've hated the thought of being tied.' She made a little expressive gesture, 'Just goes to show that we never know tomorrow, or ourselves.' She held

Lydia's gaze, her question direct, 'You wouldn't object to having Giles as a brother-in-law, would you?'

Lydia clenched her hands to disguise their trembling. *Giles and Janice!* Giles, her brother-in-law! The irony went deep. The possibility had secretly haunted her during the past weeks.

'Why, no,' she managed to say.

'Then that's fine,' Janice exclaimed with a self-satisfied air. 'Now let's get back to Noël. Your marriage to him would solve a great many problems.'

Weariness, dismay, hurt, made Lydia's expression suddenly stark. Her shoulders drooped as she whispered, tears filling her eyes, 'I'm so tired of problems, Janice – so *tired.*'

Janice countered grimly, her attitude pitiless, 'You created them; had all the answers. Don't expect any sympathy from me. And now suppose we look at this from Timothy's point of view?'

'Timothy's?' Lydia echoed fearfully.

'Yes; here's your chance to do something practical: give him a stable future. Noël loves him and the child needs a father. He's reaching the age when it's important.'

Lydia said icily, 'And you know I have no

guarantee, no matter what I might do, that Timothy's future would be secure.'

'True.' Janice spoke slowly and deliberately, 'All the same, I'll have a bet that if you were to marry Noël, you'd get all the co-operation you want, and there'd not be any problems left to worry about. It's up to you, and a question of how much you love Timothy.'

Lydia didn't speak; she just sat there numb, defeated, saying finally, 'If only I could *trust* you, Janice.'

Janice smiled, a cryptic smile. 'The important thing is that *I* can trust *you*… I'm glad we've had this little talk. Oh, hell!' as the doorbell rang.

It was Noël. Janice greeted him effusively, indicating that she was just going out and adding to Lydia, 'I'll be with Giles at the cottage if I'm needed.'

'Alone with Lydia,' Noël said, instantly aware of the tension, 'I thought I'd find out how things are.' He sat down and studied her, his gaze intent and unnerving.

Lydia regained a little of her lost courage, took a deep breath and said, 'Better for your being here.'

Noël's voice was solemn. 'The month is almost up, Lydia. Must I wait until the eleventh hour, or can I have your answer now?'

'Now,' she said quietly, but resolutely. 'My answer is yes, Noël.'

Noël looked half-believingly as he heard Lydia's words; so much so, that she managed to laugh and exclaim, 'Is the shock so great?' She told herself as she spoke that she must never condemn Noël to the suspicion that he might be second best.

'Yes,' he admitted bluntly. 'I couldn't convince myself that you would stop running away, and realize that problems are seldom insoluble.'

'I am not going to think of them at the moment,' she said truthfully. 'You know the facts, and that is all I care about.'

Noël kissed her with tenderness, realizing instinctively that she had many adjustments to make before she could relax into security and happiness. He did not automatically assume that she had suddenly fallen in love with him, but was content with the conviction that propinquity would, in time, bring that about. He recalled having told her that love had been known to grow out of affection and friendship.

'You've been marvellous to me, Noël,' she said in a rush of gratitude. 'I do so want to make you happy.'

'You can only do that by being happy yourself. No one can be happy in isolation… What do you think Timothy will say?'

Lydia didn't hesitate. 'He'll be glad. He said a little while ago that there were only "women around here".'

Noël chuckled. 'And Janice?'

Lydia vowed not to make an issue of Janice. 'She'll heartily approve. She's already told me that people are wondering when we were going to marry.'

'Really?' Noël looked delighted. 'I've been blind to everything except the possibility that you might not marry me … it's been a hellishly long wait!'

Lydia felt that she was standing beside herself, watching instead of participating. The present seemed as unreal as the past. She wondered what Giles would think, and then ridiculed herself for imagining that it would matter in the least to him. The idea of his becoming her brother-in-law was agonizing, but she argued that building a new life with Noël would absorb her interest, so that her love for Giles would, in time, fade, until she could look back and marvel that she had ever cared for him.

'How about telling everyone? Saturday

would be a good day – invite Giles and the staff for drinks?' Noël looked at Lydia for her reactions.

She agreed.

'Surprise them,' Noël went on gleefully, 'although, if what Janice says is true, that will hardly be the case, and I don't give a damn, either!' He studied Lydia reflectively. 'You're a wonderful person,' he said proudly. 'I should love you, even were I not *in* love with you.' His laugh was a little self-conscious. 'Hell! I must be sickening for something. Not used to making pretty speeches!' He reached out and clasped her hand, holding it tightly, unable to believe in his good fortune.

'I shall tell Timothy tomorrow,' Lydia said quietly, 'and say that it's to be a secret until Saturday. That will please him.'

Timothy listened solemnly to the news, his expression increasingly alarmed, his face puckering and tears filling his eyes, as he cried, 'Oh, Mummy; please don't go away – don't leave me – don't *leave* me.'

Lydia looked appalled. 'Darling,' she hastened, 'of course I'm not going away, or going to leave you.'

'Then will Uncle Noël come here to live?'

Lydia had overlooked that phase. 'Things

haven't been settled yet, but whatever happens, we shall all be together.'

Timothy brushed a hand over his eyes. 'And I'll have a daddy – like all the other boys at school?'

'Yes, darling ... you'll like that?'

He nodded, brightening. 'Will Dr Palmer still be here? I like Dr Palmer.'

'Of course.' Lydia was half afraid of what might come next, and hurried on to explain that this was to be a secret until Saturday.

'Can I tell Nanny?' The words rushed out.

'If you tell Nanny it won't be a secret, will it? This is just between *us*.'

He crinkled up his nose, eyes rounding as he promised quaintly, 'I won't even whisper it to God... But He knows secrets... Nanny says so.' Excitement crept into his voice as he rushed on, 'Will I have a brother? I'd like a brother.'

'We'll have to see ... now run along; it's nearly bath time.'

He looked up at her anxiously, fear returning. 'You'll come and tell me a story?'

'Of course I'll tell you a story.' She spoke reassuringly.

Satisfied, he smiled, and walked away.

Tears stung Lydia's eyes. At least marrying Noël could only bring stability to the situation, and as her husband, would be invaluable in any fight. Marriage would, even as he had said, strengthen her hand and perhaps, indirectly, solve her problem.

7

There was a festive atmosphere at Prior's Gate that Saturday evening. The moment Lydia had suggested to Janice that they had a few people in for drinks, Janice took over, insisting that they ought to make it a small informal party, and ask Trevor and Mark and Nina Brett, among others. Since Lydia knew that Noël was in the mood to welcome the world and his wife, she acquiesced.

Jane and Una were both baffled by the invitation, Jane insisting that there was something in the air, and that Janice was looking far too self-satisfied for anyone's good. Una suggested that it might well turn out to be an Engagement party, since Giles and Janice had lived in each other's pockets during the past weeks. Neither stressed their earlier fears for Lydia's happiness.

Giles, in turn, had no desire to go to Prior's Gate for a social evening. Working with Lydia was another matter; but Janice was persuasive, suggesting that she needed his presence to help her cope with the boredom she always felt at parties. Nevertheless, he made a point of being late, and shuddered at the waves of sound that greeted him as the front door opened, and Mrs Lane said, 'Good evening, Doctor.'

'Freezing,' he corrected, as she took his coat. Then jerking his head in the direction of the drawing room, added, 'Sounds merry!'

She beamed. 'I like to hear people enjoying themselves.'

'Good for you.' He sauntered away, glancing idly to the top of the staircase as he did so. Timothy, in dressing gown, sat knees to chin, hands clasped around his legs, on the top stair. As he saw Giles, he pursed his lips and put his forefinger against them. Giles reached him in a few strides. 'What are you doing?' he asked, smiling.

'I'm keeping a secret,' he answered in a whisper.

'Really?' Giles hunched himself down at Timothy's side.

'You won't tell Mummy I'm here – will you?'

'No; but where's Nanny?'

'Helping Ellen – in the kitchen.' He looked at Giles with a superior air. 'It's a very important secret,' he added.

'Is it?'

'Sh – h–' Timothy said, scrambling to his feet. 'Someone's coming… You won't say anything – will you?'

Giles promised; and the small figure shot out of sight. Giles returned to the hall, passing Nanny as he strolled into the drawing room.

Lydia was standing near the door as he entered. The sight of her made his heart contract and his pulse race. 'A far cry from surgery,' he said, noticing her attractive sapphire velvet dress, adorned by a diamond brooch – Noël's engagement gift. She tried to shut her ears to the sound of his voice, acutely conscious of his nearness. Their eyes met, and the gaze lingered, emotion overwhelming. In that second Giles knew he was in love with her, and had been from the beginning. Nothing that Janice had told him could alter the fact.

'You look so lovely,' he murmured tensely, deciding that neither the past, nor the present, would influence him, and that he hadn't any intention of sitting back tamely without a fight.

Lydia stared at him aghast, colour rushing to her cheeks, amazement mingling with fear.

Janice, annoyed, hurried towards them.

'Giles! You're late!'

He might not have heard her as he watched Lydia walk away. Everything around him had a dream-like quality about it. In love with Lydia! What a blind fool he'd been to waste valuable time, imagining, subconsciously, that Janice's company would suffice, and enable him to escape from reality. Determination took the place of a former anger and jealousy. He argued that Janice could be wrong about Noël. Relationships were invariably misleading. His heart thudded as he recalled the expression in Lydia's eyes a moment ago, and he relived the ecstasy that surged between them. Was it that being in love himself enabled him to recognize love in return? And hadn't Lydia always looked at him with half-concealed emotion?

'Giles!' Janice's voice was raised. 'What's the matter?'

'"Matter"?' He stared at her, his expression changing as he clicked back into an awareness of his surroundings.

'You were miles away,' she protested, irritated.

Lane appeared with the drinks tray, and Giles took a glass of champagne, his hand unsteady.

Janice watched him, unable to fathom his behaviour. He stood there in silence, oblivious of her, and actually thinking only of how he could get Lydia alone; tell her the truth, prepared to face anything, provided she returned his love.

'Quite a crowd,' he mumbled, grateful for the champagne.

'Lydia felt she owed our friends hospitality... I'd much rather be having dinner alone with you somewhere.' Janice deliberately gave him a little intimate smile.

Giles looked vague and made no comment.

Meanwhile Lydia managed to talk to the guests without anything registering. The expression in Giles' eyes haunted her. His remark about her appearance awakened momentary and undreamed of happiness. Why, suddenly, should he behave in such a manner? She dare not look at him across the room, while feeling instinctively that his gaze was upon her. Almost panic-stricken, she watched events drawing inexorably towards a climax as Noël said, 'I think now's the time to tell them – before supper?'

Lydia nodded in dumb agreement.

And suddenly there was silence as Noël announced the engagement.

‘I know you will congratulate me.’ He added, looking down at Lydia with tenderness and pride, ‘I am a very lucky man.’

Giles heard the words, staggered, every drop of blood seeming to freeze in his veins, his world crashing about him; his love doomed almost before he had time to grasp its significance.

Janice whispered in triumph, ‘Thank goodness for that. You see, I wasn’t wrong!’ She stepped forward and kissed Lydia and Noël in turn. ‘I can’t tell you how happy I am for you both. I’m thrilled, Noël! I always hoped I’d have you for a brother-in-law.’

Giles continued to stand, trance-like, until he realized that he had to say something. His voice was hollow and subdued as he exclaimed, ‘All the happiness.’

Watching, alert, Janice noticed the strain on Lydia’s face, and how she avoided actually looking at Giles, who was obviously tense and ill-at-ease. Jealousy flared and she said lightly, and with banter, ‘My sister needs someone to look after her… Ah, Trevor’ (as Trevor moved into the little circle), ‘don’t you agree, having known us both in the Tetbury days?’

Trevor, looking annoyed, mumbled something inarticulate, finishing with, ‘I agree with Noël: he is a very lucky man.'

When everyone had filed into the dining room, Janice drew Trevor into the small adjoining study.

'They'll be far too busy choosing what they're going to eat to miss us for a minute or two,' she insisted.

Trevor looked at her critically. 'Have you engineered this engagement?' he demanded startlingly.

'I? Oh, don't be so ridiculous!'

'I don't trust you.' There was a warning note in his voice.

She laughed mockingly. 'Coming from *you*–'

'Lydia's heart is not in this engagement, and you want a clear field so that you may marry Giles. It adds up. All I know is that there's something wrong *somewhere*.'

'Male intuition?' Her voice changed. 'I want you,' she said swiftly, touching his hand.

He tried to resist her, resentful of the power she exercised, but desire defeated him and his lips went down fiercely on hers.

When she drew back she said, 'Wednesday, after two.'

'No – I–'

'Wednesday,' she repeated, softly and invitingly.

'Very well,' he agreed weakly.

'I'll go back into the dining room first,' she whispered.

To her chagrin, Giles made no comment on her absence. She sensed that he had not even noticed it.

'Well,' she began, helping herself to the various dishes set out on the table. 'Now we can have some peace. I'm off the hook, Giles, with Lydia–'

He cut in sharply, 'I don't want to hear any more, Janice.'

She stared at him, resenting his tone. 'What's that supposed to mean?'

He was coolly explicit, 'The past is – *past.*'

She frowned, and noticed that he was not eating. 'Where's yours?' she exclaimed, indicating her own plate.

'I'm enjoying this claret … not hungry.'

Janice followed his gaze to where Noël and Lydia were standing, and a flame of jealousy touched her as she saw the expression in his eyes. Nevertheless, she argued, had he entertained any sentimental ideas about Lydia, her engagement had smashed his hopes, so what had she, herself, to fear? The fact that she was still sexually attracted to Trevor in no way cancelled her determination to become Giles' wife.

'Stay on after this crowd has gone,' Janice said later.

Giles was going to refuse, but then agreed.

Janice waited until the front door closed on the last guest and she, Giles, Noël and Lydia, were settled in the drawing room over a brandy, before she said, looking hard at Lydia, 'What about Timothy in all this? Don't you think he ought to have been told?'

Giles studied Lydia intently as Janice's words brought a sudden silence. He was surprised by the fire in her eyes, and was aware of the suppressed anger in her voice as she replied, 'I have already told Timothy.'

'Oh!' Janice gave a little harsh laugh, feeling raw and deflated because of Giles' attitude. 'I don't know why you and Noël have been so secretive.'

Noël countered, irate, 'There's no question of secrecy.'

'Not to worry,' Janice said airily, 'so long as Timothy knows... Security is very important to a child.'

'I don't need to be reminded of that,' Lydia retorted icily.

Just then Giles had a vision of Timothy sitting at the top of the stairs. What did the future hold for him? Giles hardly dare look at Lydia because of the overwhelming love and tenderness he felt for her, despite what Janice had told him.

'Will you continue to live here?' he asked almost abruptly.

'It hasn't been settled,' Lydia replied evasively, faint consternation in her eyes.

Noël put in, addressing Lydia, 'But I think we had a tacit understanding that you should come to Avonbury and transform it.'

Lydia nodded, remembering. 'That's true.'

Janice looked doubtful as she commented, 'I wonder how Timothy would like that… Ah, well, he could always stay here with me.' She spoke on a note of bravado before adding, 'Assuming, of course, that I wish to continue living here. There's a great deal to discuss.'

Lydia froze. Janice's words emphasized the magnitude of the problem, and she resented Janice's authoritarian manner.

Giles got to his feet, unable to bear the emotional suspense and warring elements any longer.

'I'll walk to the cottage with you – for a breath of air!' Janice exclaimed.

'It isn't a summer night,' he prompted, wanting to be alone.

'I'll come anyway,' she retorted coolly. 'Give the love-birds a little time to themselves.'

Outside, Giles was ready for attack as he faced Janice, 'If you were deliberately trying to be offensive, you certainly succeeded.' His breath was visible in the cold night air. Frost lay like snow over the landscape.

Janice, shocked, protested vigorously.

'It wasn't so much what you said, but the innuendo,' he insisted.

'You've suddenly become very sensitive to Lydia's feelings.'

'I'm sensitive to anything that involves Timothy.'

'Because of what I told you?'

'Perhaps.'

'You make no allowances for *my* feelings… Oh,' she hurried on impatiently, 'let's forget the whole miserable business. Thank heaven we're getting away from this place for a few hours tomorrow.'

'Tomorrow?' He looked vague.

'Visiting your aunt.'

Giles could not think of anything he wanted to do less than take Janice to meet his aunt, but he made some inarticulate sound and added, 'You're shivering; ridiculous to come out unnecessarily.'

Janice capitulated. A quarrel could prove disastrous. She nodded, smiled up at him, and opened the front door, turning back to say, 'Midday tomorrow.'

Giles strode away. In a matter of hours the whole fabric of his life had changed.

It was a few days later that Lydia went over to supper with Noël, with Janice on call.

Over coffee Noël said firmly, looking solemn, 'I'd like to get our plans settled.'

Plans. The word brought dread, but Lydia managed to smile encouragingly, knowing that he was referring to her moving to Avonbury, and realizing that a complete change of scene was essential.

'Will it be a wrench to leave Prior's Gate?'

'No.' Her voice was low. To her, Prior's Gate had become a habit, but never represented happiness. 'Only Timothy has roots there,' she said simply, and a pang shot through her because she knew that, without Giles, any house would merely represent bricks and mortar.

Noël was instantly alert. 'Meaning you don't think he'll want to come here?'

'No; I've already sounded him out, and once he realized that he could transfer all his belongings, and have a dog… I hope you won't mind his having a dog here, but it was a great inducement!'

'Mind!' Noël beamed. 'He could have a safari park if we had room!' There was a hesitant pause before he went on, 'What developments have there been with – with his mother? You said that you were going to pursue the matter further.'

Lydia looked down at her hands with a gesture that Noël had come to accept as a prelude to bad news. 'Nothing has changed; she flatly refuses to allow me to adopt him. My marrying you makes no difference whatsoever.' Her eyes were tear-filled as she added, 'You cannot reason with bitterness and spite.'

Noël felt the depth of her sadness and hastened, 'It may be a cliché, but one never knows tomorrow, Lydia. I don't think that woman will ever want Timothy, or the responsibility and upheaval of his suddenly appearing in her life. That's only common sense. She's been content for you to look after him from birth, and if she waits until he's older before claiming him, *he'll* have something to say in the matter.'

Lydia's control snapped; her voice broke as she cried, 'Oh, Noël, don't you see? I'm thinking of all he would have to go through before he was able to say *anything.* And unless I can adopt him he can never, legally, have his father's name.'

'Or mine,' Noël prompted. 'Once we are married, I shall have your authority to tackle her.'

'I hate burdening you with all this.'

Noël frowned. 'Don't talk like that.'

'I was told not to mention the subject again for six months. The cat-and-mouse game seldom varies.'

'Then let's accept the facts and concentrate on other important issues.' He outlined his plans for structural alterations to the house, finishing with, 'Timothy is used to space.'

Lydia hesitated, 'He will adjust, Noël. It's important for him not to have too much, or to be spoiled, because of the circumstances. That would be self-indulgence on our part, and unfair to him.'

Noël gave her an endearing smile. 'So long as *you* said it!' He added as she smiled, 'I'd like to feel that he is *our* trust.'

'You've been wonderful about it all.'

'Then be happy. Timothy's not going to be whisked away overnight.'

Lydia flushed. Just then she had been thinking of Giles. Would he have understood all this?'

Noël changed the subject, mentioning Janice and her attitude towards Lydia leaving Prior's Gate, appreciating that it would be a very large house for one person to maintain, but suggesting hopefully that she might marry and solve the problem.

'I'm sure she is keen on Giles.' Noël studied Lydia intently.

'I agree.'

'And what of his feelings?' Noël waited somewhat apprehensively. Giles' name always held significance.

Lydia felt that Giles must be standing there beside her, as on that Saturday night, when his gaze was so deep, so penetrating that it seemed they were the only two people in the room. In different circumstances she would have said he was in love with her, while, in retrospect, arguing that it was simply a question of her seeing what she wanted to see.

'Well?' Noël prompted.

'I really couldn't tell you anything about Giles' feelings.'

Noël agreed. 'He's certainly a bit of an enigma. All the same, it would be very convenient if they married and he moved into Prior's Gate.'

'Life is seldom convenient,' Lydia exclaimed with a sigh.

'But you'd be pleased if it turned out that way?'

Lydia managed to keep emotion in check as she replied, 'Naturally; as you say, it would be very convenient.'

'If you really preferred to stay on at Prior's Gate, I shouldn't make it an issue,' Noël went on, much to Lydia's surprise. 'I could sell this place ... probably be better in the long run.'

'No,' Lydia exclaimed emphatically. 'I want to get away. After all, Prior's Gate is Janice's home as much as mine, and I've no intention of sharing it with her once I'm married.'

Thus it was settled, but just before Lydia was leaving, Noël drew her into his arms and said firmly, 'We haven't fixed the date, darling. Please make it soon.'

Lydia rested weakly against him, grateful for the security of his presence, his unfailing loyalty, and aching to respond to the love she knew to be deep and unchanging.

'April – Spring. There will be quite a bit to arrange before then.' She looked up at him half-fearfully, not wanting to see disappointment in his eyes.

But Noël's reaction was immediate and relieved. He had been prepared for a much longer engagement. His kiss was swift. At this stage he had no intention of forcing an intimacy to which she could not respond.

Lydia drove the short distance to Prior's Gate through autumn mists, the tang of bonfires filling the night air. To her amazement, as she stepped into the hall, Giles came towards her from the direction of his consulting room, his presence alarming her, since Janice was on call.

'Something wrong?' she asked anxiously.

'There could well have been,' Giles admitted. 'Mrs Bellew telephoned, but couldn't get any reply.'

Consternation showed immediately on Lydia's face, 'But that's ridiculous … where was Janice? And in any case, Mrs Lane would answer.'

'Unfortunately the practice number hadn't been switched through from surgery, so Mrs Lane couldn't hear it ring.' Giles was hesitant.

'And Janice took surgery.' Lydia's voice was critical.

'Yes; I was called out on a hepatitis case.'

'Then how did *you* come to see Mrs Bellew?'

'When her husband couldn't get through he assumed the telephone was faulty, and drove here. She'd gashed her hand pretty badly, but wouldn't let Mr Bellew take her to hospital. Mrs Lane immediately telephoned the cottage and, as luck would have it, I'd just that minute got in.' He added, 'So very little time was lost, and no one had cause for complaint.'

'For which, thanks to you, we must be grateful; but that's not the point,' Lydia added, her expression grave. 'Where is Janice?'

Giles looked blank. 'Mrs Lane said she went out in a hurry. Maybe she took a call on the private line.'

'But she didn't leave a number where she could be contacted?'

'Apparently not.' Giles appreciated Lydia's insistence upon someone always being on call, and the telephone answered.

'Speculating won't solve anything ... come and have a drink.' Lydia knew it was not necessary to detain him, yet was impelled to do so.

They walked into the drawing room which glowed in the light of softly shaded lamps, and blazing log fire.

'I'll have a very small brandy,' she said,

indicating the cabinet.

He poured two. The mood changed, the mask of professionalism fell away as she sat down, excitement mounting. Giles remained standing, looking down at her from a position in front of the chimney-piece, as he raised his glass, 'To your happiness … now I shall never know the truth about you.'

She stared at him, shaken, fear in her voice as she echoed, '"The truth"?'

'Yes; you've never really told me anything about your life, Lydia.' His utterance of her name sounded like a caress; his gaze was deep and tinged with regret.

She asked breathlessly, 'Why should I have anything *to* tell?'

'Or to hide?' He pressed the question.

Her eyes, wide and honest, met his levelly, 'Would you believe me if I said that my task has been to protect other people's secrets?'

Emotion surged between them as she hung on his reply, and in that moment, doubt slipped away as Giles said hoarsely, 'Oh, yes; *yes,* I'd believe you.'

Lydia lowered her gaze, only her loyalty to Noël giving her the strength to remain silent when there was so much she wanted to say – to tell.

Just then Janice's voice, like a strident note

shattering glass, reached them from the doorway, 'Don't let me disturb this cosy little scene.'

8

Janice's nerves were raw as she saw Giles and Lydia together. Fear grew that Giles was becoming disenchanted so far as she herself was concerned. The Sunday at Ledbury had been a disaster. Giles behaved like a man in a trance, while her own frustration and intolerance of the aunt's eccentricities created an atmosphere of mutual dislike. In addition, Janice had the instinctive feeling that he doubted her story about Timothy. It wasn't what he said, but what he conveyed. And while she had the satisfaction of knowing that, initially, she had been instrumental in driving a wedge between him and Lydia (thus precipitating Lydia's engagement), nevertheless the once rosy prospect of becoming Giles' wife receded, and for the moment she had no further cards to play.

Lydia ignored Janice's melodramatic entrance and went straight to the point, outlining the facts and finishing with, 'Not only were you out when supposed to be on call, but you hadn't even switched the telephone through from surgery.'

Janice hadn't a slick answer. She had been over to Kineton, planning to make up for the unsatisfactory Wednesday visit, and deliberately not telephoning in advance in case Trevor might make an excuse not to see her. But he was out, and after waiting an hour, she had rushed back at breakneck speed, aware of the gravity of deserting her post, having completely forgotten the telephone.

'Then there's nothing I can say, is there?'

'You could give some explanation. If you'd been on an emergency, you could have transferred the calls to me.'

'I don't deny that.' Janice had no intention of making excuses.

'Patients,' Lydia insisted, 'have a right to expect that one of us is always available. You know my views on the subject. If I can't trust you to be here when you are supposed to be, then I'm entitled to an explanation.'

'I'm afraid you won't get one,' came the cool reply, 'and since Giles stood in–'

'Only by a lucky coincidence,' Giles cut in, his voice sharp.

Janice made an impatient gesture. 'The stupid woman could have gone to Casualty.'

'And we,' Lydia stressed, 'could have been reported. Quite rightly. I will not have the reputation of this practice jeopardized by your irresponsibility, *or* our patients placed at risk.'

Janice was tight-lipped. 'I'm sick to death of patients.'

'Then I suggest you give up medicine.'

Giles emptied his glass, and looked at Lydia. 'I'll be getting back to the cottage – have something to eat,' he added, remembering food for the first time.

Lydia looked shocked. She had overlooked the possibility that he might not have had supper.

Janice turned, and said with insolent mock sympathy, 'I'm *so* sorry I've deprived you of your meal.'

Giles made no reply. 'Good night, Lydia.' He went from the room.

Lydia sat back in her chair and studied Janice critically. 'You're quite insufferable; but I'm not blind. The sweetness and light of a few weeks ago – all the talk about love and Giles! I certainly see no evidence of anything remotely connected with the marriage you spoke of as a foregone conclusion.'

Janice went white with rage. 'Go to hell!'

Lydia might not have heard her, and stressed the point, 'Whatever the purpose of that little charade might have been, your schemes have obviously failed.'

Janice smirked. 'Have they?' She stared Lydia out. 'Have they? They fooled *you* at the time! I'll settle for that. If *I* can't have Giles, you certainly won't!'

Lydia went cold; events rushed up at her; memories swirled back. Just what had Janice told Giles about the past? His words, 'Now I shall never know the truth about you', echoed with a new significance. Had the remark been prompted by her own reticence, or by lies imparted by Janice which he doubted? Nevertheless, she knew that, now, she had Giles' trust, and for the moment it was enough; but apprehension built up as she looked at Janice's changing expressions, the gloating, the dark anger, the arrogance. Did Janice suspect her love for Giles? Was that it? The possibility made her shudder because it could be a weapon in Janice's hands.

'Don't degrade yourself further,' Lydia said, getting to her feet. 'I'll take the calls tonight.'

Janice glowered as she watched Lydia's retreating figure. Nothing had worked out to her own advantage, she thought fiercely. The hazard of losing Trevor reduced her to a near-panic. He fulfilled a vital sexual need, and gave her a sense of power. Of course he wouldn't be able to resist her, and his weakness added extra stimulus. Now, more than ever, she needed his attentions. When she reached her bedroom, she sat down and stared at the telephone uncertainly, then, rather frantically, dialled his number.

His voice answered pleasantly.

She said, 'Darling! I've been over to see you.'

'So I was told.'

'I can manage tomorrow.' Her heart raced.

'Make it about one.' His tone was brusque.

'Trevor–?'

'One o'clock,' he repeated. 'Good night.'

Janice manoeuvred her professional visits and arrived at Kineton on time. Trevor received her with a formality that shocked her.

'A drink?'

'Better not; I've patients to see later on, but we've got an hour,' she said eagerly, moving closer to him, dismay gripping her because his expression was icy and he made no attempt to kiss her.

'We shall not need an hour,' he exclaimed. 'I just want to tell you that we're finished, Janice – finished,' he added firmly.

She stared at him, disbelieving, not knowing whether to plead, or protest.

'Oh, don't be foolish,' she countered weakly, frightened by his calm withdrawn attitude. *'Darling–'*

He interrupted her, 'I don't want a scene; we're *finished.* I blame myself for being weak enough to start again. But that's over. You've neither scruples nor loyalty; you manipulate people for your own ends. All I hope is that Giles has the wit to see through you.' He added solemnly, 'You represent everything I despise in myself. The admission doesn't in any way absolve me from blame, but without you, I shall, at least, regain my self-respect. I've no idea what game you're playing at the moment, and I don't care. You're not going to involve me.'

She continued to stare at him, genuine panic in her eyes.

'Listen,' she began desperately, 'I love you and–'

'You've never loved anyone in your life except yourself,' he cut in coldly, 'so spare me the hypocrisy. And let's not drag out this unpleasant scene.'

She turned on him. 'If you think you can get away with this,' she threatened, adding swiftly, 'I didn't mean that – honestly I didn't.'

'Only because you haven't any weapon with which to blackmail me.'

'But why? *Why?*' She threw her arms out in a gesture of appeal.

'Something about you at Lydia's engagement party,' he replied. 'I realized just how diabolical your intentions were. To marry Giles, and keep me as your lover. What kind of a man would that make me? And when you came here on Wednesday there was not even desire left – and certainly not respect.'

Anger blazed in her eyes as abuse fell from her lips, and when at last there was silence, he walked to the door, opened it and said, 'Goodbye, Janice.'

She hesitated, then, knowing she was defeated, strode past him, tight-lipped, shaking with rage.

When he heard the car drive away, Trevor flopped down in his nearest chair, limp, a feeling of revulsion washing over him, followed by infinite relief.

Janice drove back to Tewkesbury; saw two patients, visited the hospital where a third, already in labour, had been admitted, and then returned to Prior's Gate. Una told her that Lydia was on her rounds.

'And Dr Palmer?'

'Seeing Mr Brecon.'

‘Oh, yes; I know – wife has carcinoma.’

Una sighed, ‘I don’t envy Dr Palmer his job. Mrs Brecon has very little time.’

Janice wanted to hit out, find a whipping-boy, because of her own depression. ‘Shouldn’t waste your sympathy, Mr Brecon probably has wife number two cosily lined up … let me know when he leaves; I want a word with Dr Palmer before his next patients arrive.’

Jane raised her eyebrows and flashed Una a meaning look as Janice walked away.

‘A sour mood today,’ she said.

‘I don’t think Dr Palmer will play,’ Una suggested.

‘He’d be better off having a game with a man-eating tiger.’

Una smiled. ‘I think he’s in love with Dr Vane. Can’t make up my mind about her engagement.’

‘Seems perfectly all right.’

‘Too right; that’s what worries me,’ Una retorted.

Janice went into Giles’ consulting room immediately after Mr Brecon left. Giles was sitting thoughtfully at his desk, flicking a paper-knife mechanically up and down on his blotting-pad. He looked up without speaking.

'I wondered,' Janice began tentatively, 'if I might pop in for a coffee this evening?' She waited in suspense.

'About eight-thirty.' His voice was business-like.

Janice's mood swung from despair to optimism. She was not beaten yet.

'Lydia's taking surgery.' The statement was bound up with a sudden suspicion linked with the time factor. Why couldn't it be before eight-thirty?

'I'm helping out,' Giles said smoothly. 'My bronchitic patients need watching, particularly now November's here.' He glanced at his calendar and then looked inquiringly at Janice, making it plain that he had nothing further to say.

'Eight-thirty,' she said, moving to the door.

He nodded.

Surgery was amazingly and inexplicably light that evening.

'Probably,' Giles suggested, when commenting on the fact to Lydia, 'because we've visited so many of those who would otherwise be condemned to stagger here.'

'You,' said Lydia appreciatively, 'are wonderful about that.'

'I hate a surgery full of patients who ought

to be at home in bed; it's a negation of what medicine's all about. At least, as I see it.'

'We do have a reputation for sparing people as much as we can. That's why I'm averse to using an emergency service unless we should find ourselves in an emergency situation,' she said, trying not to think of the previous evening.

But Giles' gaze rested upon her with a gentleness that made her want to cry. She heard the echo of his words, 'Oh, yes; I believe you', and lost identity in her love for him.

'I must hurry,' she managed to say, her voice shaking. 'Noël will be here before I've changed. Thanks so much for your help.'

Giles wanted to take her in his arms; ask her why her lips said one thing and her eyes, as they met his, another. Instead, he inclined his head and exclaimed, as he reached the door of her consulting room, 'Don't hesitate to transfer the calls to me if you want to go out.'

'We shan't go out this evening, and you've done enough, anyway.'

Giles gave her a long, lingering look which made her heart seem to miss a beat. She stood there, lost, unhappy, and suddenly afraid.

Noël tipped an array of brochures in her lap some short while later.

'There! Take your pick... The Greek islands; Madeira; Italian lakes; you name it, we'll be there, shaking the confetti out of our hair!'

Lydia glanced at the assortment of colours, vivid blue skies, deep blue seas, ancient buildings, palm trees, and emotion welled up, forcing her to swallow hard.

'Well?' he asked, perching himself on the arm of her chair, and suddenly freezing as he cursed himself for not remembering where she and Dennis had spent their honeymoon. In profile her face was calm, but he was aware of the tension and collected the literature with blithe inconsequence. 'On second thoughts, you tell me where you'd like to go, irrespective of all these.' He tossed them carelessly aside.

Lydia tried to think of an answer, and then said spontaneously, 'Holland. Amsterdam. Not Paris in the spring, but Holland in tulip time.'

Noël looked delighted. 'You sound enthusiastic!' he exclaimed.

'I am,' she insisted, grateful to be completely sincere. 'I've always wanted to go there, but something has prevented it.

Maybe I have some Dutch ancestors.'

Janice joined them.

'Oh, hello,' Noël said, feeling immediately deflated.

'Don't worry,' she quipped, 'I'm not staying.' She paused for a second before adding, giving Lydia a triumphant smirk, 'I'm going to the cottage. If Giles *should* ring, would you tell him that I've had to see Mrs Burns, and will come straight to him from there?... Don't look so surprised, Lydia; and have a good evening.'

'Thanks be,' Noël said, as Janice left. 'What was all that about your looking surprised?'

Lydia replied, 'I cannot read my sister's mind.' Her heart was racing and there was a sick sensation in her stomach.

Janice congratulated herself on a clever manoeuvre. And when she reached the cottage punctually at eight-thirty, she behaved as though completely at home, saying, as she relaxed in an armchair, 'Thank heaven for a little peace … this is an oasis, Giles.'

His gaze was steady and critical. 'If that is so, then you've certainly not contributed anything towards it.'

She was completely taken by surprise as she gasped, 'What do you mean?'

‘That you have been doing your best to stir up trouble.’

‘In what way?’ She played for time, so that she might work out some plan of campaign.

‘I don’t believe your story about Timothy, or anything you said about Lydia. What I am interested in is why you should want to discredit your sister.’

Janice shrank from his cutting words, but flashed back, ‘*I* can’t discredit her; she discredited *herself* years ago. I resent your tone and your accusations.’

Giles might not have heard her as he went on remorselessly, ‘I also have grave doubts about your insinuations regarding Noël’s and Lydia’s former relationship.’

Janice stared at him, totally unprepared for the additional accusation.

‘You must be mad! What difference did that make to me?’

‘None. On the other hand, I rather think you counted on it making a difference to *me*.’

Janice tried to dismiss the fears beginning to undermine her confidence, and said tartly, ‘Since she is going to *marry* Noël, I really can’t see the purpose of this conversation.’ She added quietly, ‘Really, Giles! I came here tonight to apologize for my behaviour last evening, not to be subjected to this tirade.' She looked at him as she went on persuasively, 'I thought we had a good friendship; even something more ... please don't spoil it. You must believe what you want to believe. I can't stop you, of course.'

'No,' he agreed, 'you can't stop me. I don't trust you, and our relationship can never be other than professional.'

The bitterness of being rejected twice in one day stung Janice into retaliation.

'And you don't fool *me!*' she cried. 'You won't face up to the truth about Lydia because you're in love with her. You're jealous of Noël, and you hate me for disillusioning you. Deny that, if you can.'

Giles stood there, dignified and withdrawn.

'I don't have to discuss my feelings with you. I've made my point. The subject is closed.'

'That,' Janice exclaimed cynically, 'is what you think.' Her attitude was suddenly smug, 'And Lydia will never love you – never; or break her engagement to Noël.' She shook her head, 'I'm so sorry you're being such a fool, Giles. But I can wait until I'm proved right.'

Giles sat there after Janice had gone, her

words mocking him. Could he honestly say that he had never contemplated fighting for Lydia's love, despite her engagement? Or that the possibility of making his intentions known to Noël had not occurred to him? Subconsciously, yes. Now he knew instinctively that his hopes were forlorn. He had been a fool, but not in the way that Janice implied. The realization of his feelings had come too late. And in those crucial days, Janice had dispensed her own poison. He asked himself gravely, 'What now?'

Events, however, shelved personal problems as a particularly cold and wet November brought an unusually steep rise in illness, involving the practice in an exhausting workload; and while influenza did not reach epidemic proportions, its severity brought complications. Giles was grateful to be spared social contact with Lydia and Janice, although they worked as a skilful team, each thankful for sporadic hours of sleep. It was not until mid-January that the pressure lessened just when, normally, they expected it to increase. Christmas for Giles had been a non-event, since he had willingly deputized for Lydia so that she might give all her attention to Timothy.

Lydia had equally refused to face up to the

future and her professional commitments so far as Giles was concerned. The question of the partnership had not been discussed further; but the tacit agreement about it remained. How could she now reverse her decision; and what possible excuse could she offer for wishing Giles to leave the practice? Quite apart from any stand Janice might take. In addition, it was not a matter she could discuss with Noël, who took it for granted that Giles was a fixture at Prior's Gate; thus, any false move on her part would arouse suspicion. The words, courage and responsibility, crept into her calculations, and she knew she could not disregard them. Nevertheless she did not underrate the self-control that would be needed, should she continue to work with him. But after many sleepless nights, she realized that their original bargain must be honoured. That decided, she broached the subject as a *fait accompli*, her manner deceptively composed.

Giles said swiftly, 'I've been wanting to talk to you about the future, but there hasn't been much opportunity lately.'

'We have only met – in passing!' she exclaimed.

They looked at each other with awareness – an intimate awareness.

Giles knew what he must say, but couldn't find the courage to say it. He just stood there, his gaze upon her in contemplation.

Something in the atmosphere made her apprehensive.

'What is it?' she asked, her expression fearful.

'I can't go through with the partnership,' he said solemnly, having appreciated from the moment Janice had accused him of being in love with Lydia, that he could not remain at Prior's Gate. The dangers were obvious.

'But–' She stared at him shocked, disbelieving.

'Of course I'll stay with you until you find a replacement.' He made a gesture of apology. 'I'm sorry.'

'So am I,' she whispered, the prospect of his going away seeming like a death. She managed to add, pride and loyalty assisting her, 'But of course, we must accept your decision.'

'It hasn't been made lightly. Please believe me.'

'I do.' Her sigh was deep. She felt instinctively that Janice was directly responsibility. 'Will you go back to London?' It seemed as far away as the Antipodes.

'I think so … return to hospital work. At

least doctors are needed.' If only everything he said didn't sound so trite and hollow; but he dare not allow himself to relax, or to explain.

Lydia looked down at her hands which were gripping the arms of the chair, and then, raising her gaze, she said quietly, 'A doctor of your calibre will always be needed, Giles. You are not just the clinical surgeon. I respect your kind of medicine.'

'Thank you.' He paused, then, 'I've not mentioned this to Janice.'

Janice swung into the common room at that moment, overhearing the remark and saying sharply, 'And what's that you haven't mentioned to Janice?'

Giles told her.

She gasped, 'I don't believe you. *Leaving!* Why?'

'For purely personal reasons.' His voice was cool.

It was a possibility Janice had not foreseen. She had counted on winning back Giles' esteem, believing that the period of intensive work would blot out her former deceits, and while such an idea was ridiculous, conceit enabled her to sustain it.

'Some secret love?' she taunted.

He ignored the remark.

Janice exclaimed, 'You can't leave us before the *wedding!*'

'I shall stay until a replacement is found.'

Janice gave a rather sneering laugh. 'Funny! I could have sworn you were sincere in the beginning, when you insisted that you wanted something permanent ... ah, well! We must be grateful you didn't walk out on us just recently.'

Lydia frowned.

Staring her out, Janice exclaimed, 'Don't look so devastated; no one is indispensable!' Suddenly the thrill of conquest superceded Janice's earlier reactions, as she looked from face to face, realizing that she had, after all, made sure that Giles and Lydia would never marry; thus Giles' leaving became a victory. Confidence returned.

Noël called out from the corridor before joining them. 'A gathering of the clans!'

'A parting of the ways would be more appropriate,' Janice retorted. 'Giles has decided to leave the practice.'

Noël experienced an overwhelming relief. Giles' presence had always seemed to constitute a threat, and while he trusted Lydia implicitly, he was convinced that Giles was in love with her, thus making propinquity a danger.

'Rather sudden, isn't it?' he queried. 'Has working with two women proved a strain?'

Giles wished he could lessen his depression by disliking Noël, but could not. In addition, Noël belonged at Prior's Gate, and was part of the past. So far as Lydia was concerned, she would remain a mystery, no matter what secrets she might be guarding. Theirs had been a strange inexplicable relationship and parting, for him, would mean perpetual trauma.

'Revelation would be a better description,' he replied. 'General practice is vastly different from hospital work.'

Suddenly to their consternation, Timothy, in pyjamas and dressing-gown, appeared in the doorway.

'Nanny said you were coming,' he protested to Lydia.

Lydia hurried forward, having overlooked the time. 'I'm sorry, darling.'

'I don't feel well,' he said, turning to Giles who had become his 'best friend' since the night of the engagement party. 'I've got cold water between my skin and my flesh.'

Giles studied the little figure with sudden apprehension. The description was apt for the onset of fever.

'It's very cold tonight, Timothy,' Giles said

with feigned cheerfulness.

'It isn't cold indoors, and I've been in bed.' The voice quivered slightly.

Lydia shot Giles an anxious glance. Timothy never made a fuss.

Janice exclaimed sharply, 'You ought not to be down here. What's Nanny doing?'

Timothy ignored her.

'Back to bed, darling,' Lydia said gently, 'and Dr Palmer will come up and have a look at you.' She flashed Giles an appealing glance as she spoke.

Suddenly Timothy gave a piercing cry and clutched his stomach, doubling up with pain.

Without a word, Giles lifted him in his arms and carried him to the nursery, Lydia followed.

Nanny, agitated and apologetic, explained, 'He said he wasn't feeling very well, but I knew you would be up to see him any minute, Dr Vane ... he must have gone downstairs while I was tidying the bathroom ... I can't think of anything he's eaten to upset him.'

Giles settled Timothy comfortably in bed and began to examine him.

Timothy looked up pleadingly from the pillows and begged, 'Please make me better,

Dr Palmer.'

'Don't worry, old chap; I will. But you must help me.'

'How?'

'By doing as you're told.'

'Oh! … I thought I felt sick, but I don't really feel sick.'

His temperature was subnormal. Giles and Lydia exchanged glances, each reading the other's thoughts. There was no evidence of appendicitis.

Janice joined them, saying superciliously, 'I do happen to know *something* about children.'

Timothy rolled his head from side to side. 'I want Mummy and Dr Palmer … please go *away*.'

Giles said with gentle firmness, 'And I want *you* to go to sleep after Nanny has given you something to make you better.'

'Medicine?'

'Yes.'

Timothy sighed a pathetic little sigh of acceptance, glancing at Lydia for reassurance.

Lydia felt cold and shaky. Timothy had never really been ill, and seeing him lying there, pale and listless, emphasized the vulnerability of her position regarding him.

A few minutes later, going into the day nursery, she looked at Giles appealingly, 'What do you think is wrong?'

Giles admitted honestly, 'At this moment I can't tell. He could be sickening for something; or he could be racing about tomorrow as though nothing had happened.'

'Hardly a brilliant summing up,' Janice observed, having joined them.

'I'm not trying to be brilliant,' Giles retorted, irritated. 'I'll get Nanny to give him a little milk of magnesia.' He didn't add that he was not satisfied with Timothy's condition, while not having any evidence to justify, or support, the reaction. An immediate diagnosis was not always a simple matter where children were concerned.

'Then suppose we don't build up the drama,' Janice suggested. 'He's probably shamming to attract attention.'

'You know that's not true,' Lydia protested.

Noël appeared anxiously in the doorway, his solicitude obvious as he moved to Lydia's side.

Giles detached himself and had a word with Nanny, prescribing the exact amount of milk of magnesia and water. A minute or two later, he and Lydia waited while

Timothy drank it.

'I shall call … my dog…'

But Timothy was asleep before uttering the name.

'Splendid,' Giles murmured.

Lydia lifted Timothy's arm and placed it between the sheets. But her fears didn't lessen.

'I'll come up again a little later, Nanny,' Giles said quietly.

When they gathered downstairs, Janice made no attempt to conceal her animosity towards Giles; the fact of his resignation inducing a fierce anger, largely because she was powerless to stop him.

'I see no reason why you should remain. Lydia and I managed perfectly well before you came here, and shall do so long after you've gone.'

Noël looked shocked, and made an exclamation of protest.

Lydia spoke up, her voice commanding. 'I'm more than grateful for Giles' help.'

'All this *fuss*. Timothy twists you round his little finger.' She added darkly, 'But you won't be able to protect him much longer. I should reconcile myself to that if I were you.'

9

Giles returned to Prior's Gate before seven o'clock the following morning. Lydia rushed to him, ashen-faced, having just telephoned the cottage.

'Thank God you're here,' she cried desperately, as Timothy's screams echoed from the nursery.

Giles, alarmed, rushed up the stairs, two at a time, Lydia hurrying behind him.

Timothy was lying on his back, his legs drawn up to his abdomen.

Examining him, Giles could feel a sausage-like swelling, with peristalsis (a wave-like movement of the intestine) visible.

'You … promised … better.' The words came between spasms of pain. Timothy's pleading, half-reproachful eyes made Giles' heart contract.

'I will make you better,' Giles hastened, looking across the bed to Lydia. 'Atropine,' he said urgently.

Lydia rushed downstairs and returned with the hypodermic and drug necessary for the injection.

'Just a little prick,' Giles said with soothing reassurance, completing the task almost before Timothy was aware of it.

Leaving Nanny to watch, Giles guided Lydia from the room.

'It's the folding of one part of the intestine into another and means immediate surgery,' he said swiftly.

Lydia gave a little gasp, fully aware of the dangers.

Giles added with urgency, 'I'll call an ambulance, and then arrange with Matron at Hill House about the theatre. If possible, I'd like Dr Baker to give the anaesthetic, then–'

Lydia interrupted, 'But you'll operate … I don't want anyone else.' She looked at him pleadingly. 'Oh, *please,* Giles.'

Their gaze met for a split second.

'Very well … you stay with him while I telephone. The atropine will act as part of the pre-med.'

When the ambulance arrived, Giles gathered a now drowsy Timothy into his arms.

'Trust me,' he whispered to Lydia. 'Everything will be ready, and Dr Baker will be there.'

'I'll come the moment Janice gets back

from her midder.' She followed them out of the house, carrying Timothy's little case which seemed to have a poignancy all its own and watched the ambulance doors close, standing in the grey, raw January morning, lost to time and place. She was no longer the efficient doctor, but the 'mother' wanting to be there, even though appreciating she could only sit and wait in that world of activity, where split seconds saved life and skilful hands sometimes worked miracles.

Janice's car turned into the drive and braked sharply.

'What on earth are you doing out here at this hour? Bad enough to have to go out myself.' She stopped, arrested by the expression on Lydia's face, and her frightening stillness. 'Something wrong? You look ghastly!'

They went into the hall. Lydia didn't want to talk, or even to tell her about Timothy, but she managed to do so, not prepared for Janice's outburst, '*Giles* operating! Why Giles? Robert Sinclair's the man.' She paused, then, 'And I don't suppose it occurred to you to contact the *mother?* She does happen to be the *next of kin*, and her consent–'

Lydia cut in icily, 'I'm not interested in her *consent*, and I'll fight if there's any trouble...

Now, if you'll look after things here, I'm going to Hill House.'

'What on earth for? They'll have him on the table as quickly as possible ... who's giving the anaesthetic?'

'Dr Baker.'

'At least he's a good choice.'

Lydia made no comment. She went upstairs and spoke to Nanny; telephoned Noël, promising to contact him later; then, grabbing a coat, went out to get her car.

Mrs Lane ran after her, appearing just as Lydia was driving from the garage.

'Oh, Doctor! You *will* let us know,' she begged, almost in tears.

Lydia promised.

'The poor little mite.'

Lydia swallowed hard, and put her foot down on the accelerator.

'Oh God, help him,' she prayed. 'Please save him.'

Lydia felt unreal as she walked into Hill House a short while later. Everything seemed strange and unfamiliar.

Nurse Smith, whom she knew quite well, came forward and said, 'Timothy is still in the theatre. Sister Jenkins said would you go along to her office?'

Sister Jenkins got up from her desk as

Lydia entered.

'I thought you'd prefer to wait in here,' she said sympathetically. 'A cup of tea?'

'Oh, please.' Lydia's mouth was dry; she spoke with difficulty. She had always appreciated the desperation of waiting parents; now she was experiencing it herself. When the tea was brought, her hand shook so much that she could hardly get the cup to her lips.

'Children have amazing resilience,' Sister Jenkins observed encouragingly.

Lydia knew that to be true, but she could still see Timothy's little pinched face and hear his cries. Taking a deep breath she looked at Sister Jenkins, comforted by her calm, gentle face. The minutes ticked by. Lydia's gaze was fixed on the door, and every time it opened, her heart seemed to stop in fear; but at last Giles appeared, still gowned up, knowing where Lydia would be waiting.

'So far so good,' he said swiftly. 'He's come through it very well.'

Sister Jenkins left them.

Lydia couldn't speak for a moment; she just stared at Giles, tears in her eyes. Then she murmured, 'Thank you; *thank* you.'

Giles wanted to hold her, comfort her; but

all he said was, 'I'll get out of this clobber.' A thought occurred to him. 'Of course, I came here in the ambulance and haven't my car! Will you give me a lift?' He hurried on, 'Work is the best thing … we know he won't be round for a while.'

Lydia nodded.

The drive back to Prior's Gate was made almost in silence, but in that silence was a depth of understanding.

'I'm so grateful I could operate,' Giles said as they stopped at the house.

'So am I.' She met his gaze for the first time.

His hand reached out and clasped hers for a brief moment. It was the touch of sympathy, reassurance; and, to him, of unspoken love.

Janice came out of her consulting room immediately after Giles and Lydia entered the hall.

'Well?' Her voice was clipped.

Giles told her, and then went through to the practice quarters.

'Just so long as he doesn't develop a paralytic ileus,' Janice suggested deliberately.

Lydia winced.

'That is not an inevitable complication after an abdominal operation,' she countered.

'True; but it is always a possibility.' Janice's eyes narrowed, her lips tightened. 'At least you've had the good sense not to hang around the nursing home all day.'

Lydia explained that she would keep in constant touch, and go back in a couple of hours, after she had seen two very sick patients.

'I shall look in sometime,' Janice announced unexpectedly. 'Oh, Noël has been in and out of here like a yoyo. I think he was rather upset that you didn't call him earlier. Rightly so, in my opinion.'

'Noël isn't a doctor,' Lydia replied quietly. 'Every second was vital. You know that, and so does he... Are you deliberately *trying* to be unpleasant and obstructive? I should have thought even you would have had a little heart in the circumstances.'

'Then you thought wrong.'

Noël appeared hurriedly, snatching a minute between appointments. He looked slightly ruffled, his voice pitched on a note of interrogation rather than sympathy, as he inquired after Timothy, and when told the facts, insisted that he ought to have been called. He was her fiancé, and Timothy would soon be his stepson.

All Lydia said wearily was that at the time

the only thing that mattered was getting Timothy to the nursing home, and then following him. Had he, Noël, been there, he could not have done anything. 'I could have waited *with* you,' he repeated stubbornly.

'Please don't let's argue.' Her voice was thin and exhausted; she seemed to have lost weight in a matter of hours.

'I'm sorry,' he apologized. 'I just resented Giles taking over.'

'But he's a *surgeon*. You know an intussusception – it can't wait for personal feelings to be taken into account. Thank God Giles was here!'

'I know; but I'll come with you to see Timothy later on.' He spoke finally.

'This evening,' she said. 'But I shall go along before then – after I've dealt with the patients.'

'Very well,' he agreed reluctantly, wanting to mention Giles, but refraining. Obviously, he would, of necessity, be looking in to see his patient. Noël despised his own jealousy, but could not curb it, and was thankful that Giles was leaving the practice.

Lydia managed to get to the nursing home just before midday. A nurse keeping vigil moved from her chair by Timothy's bedside, and together they looked down at the tiny figure, made doubly pathetic by the blood-drip and Ryles feed-tube inserted in his nose. Lydia felt that some part of her was lying there – a wounded part, for which there was no palliative.

Sister Jenkins joined them, and Lydia said, trying to steady her voice, 'You *will* keep him sedated after the anaesthetic has worn off?' She hastened apologetically, 'I know you will, but–'

'Don't worry,' Sister Jenkins assured her, 'he won't know anything, or anyone, today… Dr Palmer has already been in. I'm so glad this is his case.'

'Yes… Dr Hunt–' She paused.

'Oh, Dr Hunt looked in.' Sister Jenkins considered Dr Hunt's attitude most odd; it seemed cold, almost callous.

Lydia did not comment, but made a little gesture of gratitude as she thanked Sister Jenkins and the nurse, gave a long lingering look at Timothy, and said, 'I'll come back later.' With that she hurried out into the corridor, and so to her car. Sitting motionless in the driving seat, fearing a spectre beside her, she recalled Janice's words of the previous evening: 'But you won't be able to protect him much longer. *I should reconcile myself to that if I were you.*' She fought against tears. There was nothing she could do. Noël knew the facts, but he seemed suddenly very far away; lost to her.

The long day dragged into late evening. She and Noël made their last visit to the nursing home, and returned to Prior's Gate. Giles called in with his final report.

'And now,' he added, addressing Lydia, 'you *must* get some rest. It's essential.'

Janice shot him a resentful glance.

Noël said, 'Giles is right. You can't have had any sleep last night.'

Giles hastened, 'A mild sedative would be a good idea. I shall be in touch with Night Sister.' He stopped, aware of Janice's expression as she got up out of her chair, turning on Lydia, eyes glaring.

'*You* need a sedative; *you* must rest.' The words came violently and with hatred. 'Well, the charade's over.' She turned to Noël and Giles, 'Timothy's *my* child! *I'm* his mother. She's a sham; soaking up all the sympathy, sitting there, pale and tragic!'

Lydia, horrified, cried, 'Oh, Janice!'

Giles sat transfixed, finding it impossible to assimilate the truth in a matter of minutes, his exclamation one of shock and disbelief.

Janice flashed Noël a defiant glance, 'I

assume *you* knew that?'

Noël, staggered by the revelation, replied icily, 'I knew only that Lydia was not Timothy's real mother.'

'Loyal to a fault,' Janice sneered. 'Thank you for nothing, Lydia. When Timothy comes out of the nursing home I shall take him away for a convenient convalescence and never come back.' She paused, then added with triumph, 'And there's nothing whatsoever you can do to stop me!'

Giles rapped out, 'You may be his mother, but he is my patient, and I shall have some say as to what is best for him.'

'True; while he *is* your patient. My sister evidently didn't trust you enough to take you into her confidence.'

Giles felt the sting of those words. Equally, he recalled what Lydia had said about keeping other people's secrets.

Lydia, petrified, asked poignantly, 'Why, Janice? Why have you chosen to say all this now?'

Janice poured out a brandy for herself. 'Because I'm sick of my life here, and because I am growing to hate the child through you. You've been in command; made the decisions; even to giving your consent for the operation. I haven't counted.'

Lydia made a helpless gesture. 'But you've never been interested in him; shown the slightest affection for him. And never wanted him!'

'That's true,' Janice admitted. 'And your noble gesture in standing by me is responsible for all the trouble. I'm sick, too, of being grateful, and of living in your shadow. To say nothing of your perpetual plea to adopt Timothy so that you could give him Dennis' name. Your husband's name.' She waited a second before looking at Noël, 'Did she tell you that Dennis was Timothy's father?'

'Yes.' Noël stared at her, appalled.

'And that shatters you, doesn't it, Giles? I can see by your expression. It isn't every day that a woman loves her husband so much she is prepared to take his mistress' child.'

Jealousy was like fire in Janice's blood at that moment. Lydia; always Lydia! Dennis loved her. And now Giles.

'I think,' said Giles, taking command, 'that you've said enough. I just want to make it quite clear that until Timothy is fully recovered, it would be highly dangerous to change the pattern. His security lies in his present relationships.'

Janice stared at him insolently. 'Very well;

I see your point about Timothy being fully recovered, but I want to make it equally clear that, after then, I shall be leaving here *for good* and taking him with me.'

The door shut.

Lydia knew she could not get to her feet, because there was no strength left in her legs. Noël crossed to her side, and shot Giles a look which suggested that his presence was unnecessary.

Giles hesitated as he met Lydia's gaze – an unconsciously pleading gaze. Then, murmuring a somewhat inarticulate 'good night', went swiftly from the room.

Lydia bowed her face in her hands.

'Why didn't you tell me it was Janice?' There was a note of faint reproach in Noël's voice.

'I couldn't betray my own sister.'

'She betrayed you.'

Stricken, Lydia cried, 'Oh, Noël; I just can't bear it.'

Noël had no words of consolation. Death seemed to lie upon the house.

10

Lydia felt that she was walking about in an abstract world during the following week. The foundation of her life crumbled; hope disappeared and courage deserted her as she thought of the future. And while Timothy was progressing, each time she saw him she had to fight back the tears. Everything that was said had some hurtful connotation; his bravery and fighting spirit doubly touching, when she contemplated all that lay ahead.

Janice was coolly self-assured. She had issued her ultimatum, and there was nothing more to be said. Lydia tried to discuss the situation and the ramifications inseparable from it, only to be told that she, Lydia, could invent what story she chose to account for the break-up. 'I shall be away from it all,' Janice said finally. 'I intend living in Scotland, Timothy will love it. A "widow" with a small son always invites sympathy. Don't worry; I have everything planned. Children are resilient creatures, with very short memories … distract their attention; give them a new toy, as it were – simple! *You* look on the verge of a breakdown.'

Meanwhile the practice continued to run normally, Giles and Lydia both thankful for the panacea of work. Giles avoided Janice whenever possible, but on this particular morning she walked into his consulting room and said boldly, 'I'm going to see Timothy, so don't expect me to examine any of your patients.'

'They would have to be in dire need of an obstetrician for me even to contemplate doing so.'

Janice ignored that, and went on smoothly, 'Sister tells me that Timothy's had bowel sounds this morning.' Her manner was superior.

Giles retorted curtly, 'I'm fully aware of my patient's condition.'

Janice studied him. 'You despise me,' she said unexpectedly.

He looked at her long and contemptuously, 'I think you are the most diabolical woman I've ever had the misfortune to meet. Quite apart from the truth about the past – your fabrications in order to revile Lydia–'

She interrupted, 'All the same, they shook you… And now–' her attitude changed, 'I want to know when Timothy is likely to be leaving hospital.'

Giles stared her out.

'When I say so, and not before.' With that he got up from his desk and left her standing there.

Lydia appeared in the doorway, having missed Giles.

'Oh,' she cried, seeing Janice.

'If you're thinking of going to the hospital this evening – *don't.* I shall be there.'

Lydia said firmly, 'Timothy is expecting me as usual. You won't make a scene in front of the nurses.'

Timothy was propped up against the pillows when Lydia arrived. He pointed to his nose and arm, and told her that he'd had the 'pipes', as he called them, taken out and that they'd had to wait for his 'tummy to make sounds'. A fact that amused him. There was no whining, merely relief and the confidence that came from feeling a little better. He added that Aunt Janice had been to see him and brought him a puzzle. He indicated it as it lay on the bed-table.

Lydia glanced at it. The picture was of Scotland.

'You look sad, Mummy. Why do you look sad? I'm *better.*'

Lydia managed to give a little laugh. 'I'm sad because I'm happy.'

He studied her thoughtfully. It didn't make sense, but he accepted it, and in a few minutes fell asleep, just as Noël joined her.

'I've a colleague I must see,' Noël explained apologetically. 'With luck, I can get to Prior's Gate later on – can't guarantee the time.'

Lydia suggested that it would be a good idea if they didn't make any plans for the rest of the evening. She would have supper on a tray and go to bed early. Even have supper in bed. She ached for the opportunity of being alone, instead of being utterly lonely among people. She wanted to escape from eyes that met hers with concern, and a degree of surprise because, now that Timothy was recovering, she should be looking better.

'Are you sure?' Noël spoke gently.

'Quite sure. I'll try to relax and – sleep.'

They parted outside the nursing home and went to their respective cars.

Back at Prior's Gate, Mrs Lane said that Dr Hunt was out, and had left a message saying that she would not be back until late. 'But Dr Palmer is in his consulting room... He told me that Timothy was going along splendidly. Nanny and I had a little weep together.'

Lydia had forgotten Nanny, and the thought of her brought back overwhelming misery; she, too, loved Timothy, and had looked after him since he was six months old, her devotion and loyalty absolute.

'Tears and happiness,' Lydia managed to say, realizing that she had never really known the meaning of happiness, and while not the crying type, had shed more tears recently than she cared to admit.

'We'll soon have him home again,' Mrs Lane went on, beaming. 'Now, what can I get you? You *must* have a proper supper.'

'A little later,' Lydia hastened. 'I must speak to Dr Palmer before he leaves, to let him know I'm back on duty.'

She went along to Giles' consulting room.

Lydia sat down in the patients' chair. Her hands dropped into her lap.

'What am I going to *do,* Giles?' Pretence vanished; the appeal was direct and unselfconscious.

'I don't know,' he answered. 'I've looked at it from every possible angle. Even now I can't grasp it all.'

Lydia hastened, her expression apprehensive, 'But you understand?'

‘Yes. And looking back to the night Timothy was taken ill, I recall Janice saying that you would not be able to protect him much longer, and that you should reconcile yourself to the fact. It struck me at the time as being strange, but Timothy’s condition put it out of my mind.’ He paused, ‘Had you anticipated her decision – been prepared for it in any way?’

‘I’d always lived under the threat, and prayed that she would eventually allow me to adopt him. If anything upset her, or she couldn’t have her own way, she immediately talked of taking him away. I suppose I deluded myself that, since she had no love for him, it was unlikely she would really want to look after him, or face up to the facts of her own position.’

‘Moral blackmail,’ Giles said in disgust. There was a moment of tense silence before he added, ‘There was one thing she said that impressed me.’

Lydia asked in a breath, ‘What?’

‘Her reference to your love for your husband.’ Giles’ voice was low. ‘You must have loved him very deeply, Lydia.’

Lydia did not avoid Giles’ steady gaze as she answered, ‘Not in the sense that you mean. I was not in love with him, Giles. I suppose my affection enabled me to show him the kindness of compassion. His remorse was so great, and he was dying. I don't know if I could have shown such magnanimity had I been deeply in love with him… That probably doesn't make much sense to you.' She spoke wearily.

Giles sat down again. 'Oh, yes; it makes sense,' he agreed quietly. 'There's no hatred, violence, or jealousy in affection. With love there can be all three.'

Lydia dare not look at him; their affinity was absolute in that moment.

Giles said abruptly, 'Tell me just one other thing: was Janice, even indirectly, instrumental in your becoming engaged to Noël?'

Lydia started, surprised and afraid of the question. She had agreed to marry Noël for various reasons which she could not specify. But her thoughts raced back to a scene when Janice was hoping to marry Giles. Janice always talked in the third person when it came to Timothy, and Lydia recalled her words when the subject of Noël and marriage was being discussed: *'I'll have a bet that if you were to marry Noël, you'd get all the co-operation you want, and there'd not be any problems left to worry about. It's up to you, and a question of how much you love Timothy'.*

Lydia said, colour rising to her cheeks, 'I'd rather not answer that question.'

Giles looked down at his desk. 'You have already done so.'

There was a finality in his manner which brought a bleak feeling of dismissal.

'I'm keeping you.' Lydia got to her feet. 'All the talking won't change the situation. But thank you for listening – and for everything.'

He held her gaze with sudden tenderness. 'You know you never have to thank *me*.'

She made no comment; control slowly deserting her.

'I shall be looking in at Hill House before I go to bed ... please have something to eat and–'

'I know,' she said with a wan smile, as she reached the door, 'get some sleep!'

'Sensible but fatuous words,' he commented.

The house seemed uncannily silent as she went upstairs. A silence which Timothy's absence had brought.

Nanny came out of the nursery as Lydia reached the landing. 'We shall soon have him home, Dr Vane. I can't tell you how much I've missed him. So amusing and full of fun.' Her smile was half-shy, and apologetic. 'He's said some of the funniest things, even at the nursing home. It's amazing for such a small child. But, then, he's so intelligent, too...' Here was pride in her voice. 'I hope you have a good night. If there's anything you want–'

'Thank you, Nanny.'

'Really, all we want is to have him back in his own bed.' She stopped; Lydia's expression distressed her. Come to think of it, Dr Vane didn't seem able to rejoice over Timothy's progress; in fact she was near to tears every time his name was mentioned. Nanny couldn't help exclaiming, 'Is something wrong?'

'No; no, Nanny – thank you.' Lydia managed to smile, and went into her bedroom. The fact that she could not fight, and was completely at Janice's mercy, filled her with sudden explosive anger and bitterness. This was not a case where she could make friends with grief; or face imminent disaster with fortitude. Even her engagement became a meaningless convention.

Mrs Lane brought her up a dainty meal, which didn't tempt her, but which she ate because of the effort and care that had gone into preparing it.

Noël telephoned her just as she was about to switch off the light. If she was feeling restless, and hadn't yet gone to bed, he could come over. She was relieved to be able to tell him that she was already in bed, appreciative of his solicitude.

Two seconds after she had replaced the receiver, the telephone rang again. She answered it, fear paralysing the muscles of her throat.

But it was Giles.

'I knew you weren't asleep.'

'How?'

'I've just driven past the house. Your light was on… I've come from Timothy.' Giles couldn't add that Timothy had asked him why *he* couldn't be his daddy – much to the nurse's amusement. Fortunately, sleep had prevented further cross-examination.

'He's all right?'

'In good form for a few minutes. Throat's a little sore, but that's after the Ryles. I've prescribed a linctus, anyway… Have you eaten?'

In that moment Lydia allowed herself to listen to his voice, its magnetism no less because of the unhappiness surrounding her. But soon, she thought in sudden panic, he, too, would be gone.

'Lydia … did you hear what I said?'

'Yes; and I have eaten.'

'Good.'

'Thank you for ringing.'

'It's not very difficult,' he said hoarsely. 'I'll see you tomorrow.'

Lydia relaxed, and stole that moment from relentless time.

It was impossible to fathom Janice's thoughts during the next fortnight. She worked as usual, was pleasant to Jane and Una, polite to Giles, while, as far as possible, ignoring Lydia. No word was said about the future, until the evening before Timothy was due to come out of Hill House. She, Lydia and Giles were in the common room after a heavy surgery when each had been available.

'How long before I can take Timothy to Scotland?' Janice addressed Giles, her manner overbearing.

'At least another two months,' he said firmly.

'Oh, don't be ridiculous!'

'You asked me; I have told you. I shall not give my consent before then, and even so, the upheaval will be traumatic for the child. The responsibility for *that* will be yours,' he finished curtly.

'A child is always better off with his mother,' she insisted.

'In normal circumstances I would agree,

but you merely gave birth to Timothy; Lydia has been his mother.'

'Two months,' Janice said icily. 'Thanks.' She walked away, and then returned. 'That will bring us to April,' she reminded Lydia. 'Couldn't be better; you'll be on your honeymoon. Between now and then, I shall begin to do more for Timothy. If Nanny doesn't like it, she can go.'

Giles looked at Lydia; neither spoke. Lydia thought desolately: What was there to say?

Timothy came out of the nursing home, weak, but bright-eyed and excited, clinging to Nanny's hand and Lydia's, and saying that his legs wouldn't go the same way as his body. Janice had wanted to collect him, but Giles had overruled her, insisting that the child needed the presence of those most familiar.

'I'm home!' Timothy cried, looking around him. 'It feels *funny.*' He beamed at Giles who was standing in the hall to greet him. 'I can stay up?'

'Yes; but you must go to bed this afternoon.'

Timothy didn't protest. 'Can I have an egg custard, Nanny? And sponge cake and soup?' He wrinkled up his nose.

Janice went forward and stooped to greet him. Timothy solemnly kissed her cheek. 'Thank you, Aunt Janice, for coming to see me, and the aeroplane and things.' His expression was that of reassessment. He liked Aunt Janice better now. She was different. Looking back at Giles, he said, 'You've made me better! But you didn't *tell* me I should have an operation.'

'You didn't tell me you were going to have a pain in your tummy!'

'My tummy itches. When can I go on my pony?' He added gleefully, 'I'm home; I don't want to go away again. Promise I shan't have to?'

He jabbered on as they put him on the sofa before the fire in the drawing room. Janice hovered. Lydia clung as much to Timothy's hand, as he to hers. It was symbolic.

'I'll stay with him,' Janice said firmly. 'I know you two have patients,' she added, addressing Giles and Lydia. 'And you must have quite a bit to do, Nanny.'

Timothy looked startled. 'I want Nanny here.'

'You can't have everything you want!' Janice exclaimed.

He stared at her. 'Now you're all horrid again; you've got that *look* on your face.'

Tears welled into his eyes; the little bubble of happiness vanished.

'Nanny will stay,' Giles promised him quietly.

'Can I have some hot milk, and honey, and a biscuit?' He sighed suddenly, and put his head back against the cushions. Exertion and excitement silenced him for a while.

Outside the room, Giles cautioned Janice, 'I should have thought even you would have had more sense than to start giving orders, before the child has had time–'

'Oh,' Janice interrupted, 'you make me tired. I won't have him molly-coddled. I've every intention of beginning as I mean to keep on.'

'So have I,' he countered sternly, 'and I'm still in charge.'

But the next month was a nerve-racking ordeal, as Janice tried to insinuate herself more and more into Timothy's life, criticizing Nanny, planning 'treats' which she decided Timothy would like, and which interfered with his routine, until one day, screaming, he told her to go away.

'I hate you,' he cried. 'You spoil things. My nanny hates you, too … yes she *does!*'

It was Giles who always came to the rescue, aware of Lydia's desperate unhappiness in face of Janice's slow, remorseless attempt to take command. Periodic tantrums took the place of laughter in the nursery, making every issue a clash of wills. Janice was incompetent and inadequate, without any idea of child psychology, using discipline as a weapon in an effort insidiously to break Timothy's spirit, while succeeding only in making him a rebel. The more Lydia tried to reason with her, the greater her aggression, while Nanny, baffled by the turn of events and Janice's persistence, struggled to placate Timothy.

And at last, Giles said adamantly, 'Janice, this situation cannot go on.'

He, Noël, Lydia and Janice were at the coffee stage after lunch one Sunday, and his attitude of grim determination brought immediate silence.

Janice looked from face to face, her expression resigned.

'Giles is right,' she said, staggering them, 'I can't become maternal overnight. What's more, I don't really want to… I've manoeuvred and maligned you, Lydia; and now I've run out of hatred.'

Lydia stared at her, hardly daring to breathe. 'What do you mean?'

'That I've no desire to look after Timothy.

I hadn't a clue what was involved in taking care of a child, or the patience it needed. I've marvelled at your love for him.' She paused. 'Oh, I'm not a reformed character, and I've no intention of making out that I am. I could no more go to Scotland and accept the responsibility of Timothy, than I could fly Concorde. He's all yours, Lydia. You can adopt him with my blessing. There's no sacrifice in the gesture, believe me. Just relief.'

Lydia, bewildered, incredulous, gasped, 'Do you really *mean* that?'

'I mean it all right... I've given you a bad time; perhaps that has been part of my revenge.'

'Revenge for what?'

'The fact that Dennis loved you. I deluded myself that he loved me. I wanted a child to force his hand – tie him. I suppose you've been a constant reminder of my own disloyalty. I wasn't big enough to appreciate your kind of compassion, and generosity. I blamed you because, after Dennis died, I didn't have a termination; although I knew I'd left it too long. You've protected me; done everything possible, but I still wanted to hurt you. Life had robbed me of the one thing I wanted – Dennis. And you were his wife, and then his widow. You were always identified with him. Not I.' She looked at Giles. 'You were quite right when you called me "a diabolical woman". When it comes to it, I love only myself. Not a pretty picture.'

Giles stared at her, speechless and thankful.

Noël asked, 'What are you going to do now?'

'Leave you all in peace,' she said calmly, and then, addressing Giles, added, 'Will you stay on here, so that the practice maintains stability?'

Noël hung on Giles' reply. Lydia dare not think, or even look at him.

'That rather depends,' Giles said slowly.

'On what?' Janice insisted, aware of his conflict and her own guilt.

Giles looked at Lydia, then at Noël, and back to Lydia.

'Recently,' he pointed out, 'there has been complication for each of us. Life here has been a façade; a process of concealment, and I don't think it is an adult way in which to face the future. By trying to spare others we all too often ruin their happiness, as well as our own.'

'What do you mean – "spare others"?' Noël demanded. 'Why don't you answer

Janice's question?'

'Very well, I will... My staying here depends on Lydia. You see, I love her; and I believe she loves me. I'd rather say this in front of you, Noël, than behind your back.'

There was amazement and incredulity in the silence that followed, before Lydia echoed, 'Love me?' Her voice was low; her eyes suddenly glowing.

Noël's sigh was audible. 'I think you have your answer, Giles.'

Giles moved to Lydia's side. 'Have I?' He looked down at her possessively.

'Yes,' she whispered. Then, 'I'm sorry, Noël; so sorry.'

Noël shook his head.

'I always knew, but refused to see,' he confessed. 'It's true – where emotion is concerned we are rarely adult.'

Janice seemed to take stock of them as she said, 'I always knew, too. My schemes didn't work, or deserve to. Now I shall go to Scotland; probably get a hospital job. Prior's Gate will be a much happier place without me.' She stated a fact, and didn't expect to be contradicted, but just then loneliness engulfed her. Hatred and bitterness had filled her heart during the past years; now she had to build a new life. She glanced at

Noël, intimating that Giles and Lydia had no need of their presence. On the way out of the room she paused and put a hand on Lydia's shoulder. 'I'm sorry; forgive me if you can.'

Alone, Giles looked at Lydia, his voice full of emotion, as he said, 'I love you, my darling. I couldn't let you go.'

He moved to sit on the arm of her chair.

Their gaze met and lingered. He lowered his lips to hers, holding her with passion, and then tenderness, and when she drew back, asked, 'When did you know how you felt about me?'

'When I tried to persuade myself that we ought to have an older man in the practice! At least, that is when I ought to have known. I didn't admit it until some time afterwards.'

'I wouldn't admit it, either… It was the night of the engagement party.'

'I wondered; but wasn't sure.'

'And now?'

'My heart knows,' she said.

He held her hand tightly. Happiness and hope made words unnecessary.

'Timothy,' she began, breaking the silence.

Giles looked into her eyes, a smile on his lips. 'He has already asked me why I can't be his daddy!'

'No! When?'

'In the nursing home.'

They laughed together.

'These weeks will not have done any real damage?' Lydia wanted to be reassured.

'No; but they've shown his spirit and character. He's a fine little chap,' Giles said fondly. 'We must see that he has a brother or a sister to play with – after we're married, of course.'

Lydia looked up at him.

'That won't be difficult,' she said.

The publishers hope that this book has given you enjoyable reading. Large Print Books are especially designed to be as easy to see and hold as possible. If you wish a complete list of our books please ask at your local library or write directly to:

Dales Large Print Books
Magna House, Long Preston,
Skipton, North Yorkshire.
BD23 4ND